This dance seemed **education in itself, for he taught her something unknown—that a palm on the small of her back could cause a tension so low in her stomach.**

"Look at me, Anna," he said and she had to peel herself from his chest to do so, but oh, he was stunning.

Sebastián Romero was, quite simply, the most beautiful man she had seen in the flesh. She wanted to kiss him and dreadfully so.

"We would move very well together."

She frowned, unsure if she'd misread the inference, but no, she looked into black eyes that beckoned bed.

"Excuse me!" Anna said, affronted, or rather trying to be, because in his arms she didn't quite know who she was. "I leave tomorrow."

"That gives us tonight."

If it had been anyone else she'd have turned on her heel and walked off, or slapped his cheek, or...

But it wasn't anyone else.

He made the incomprehensible, a one-night stand, somehow sensible.

Heirs to the Romero Empire

A brand-new sizzling Spanish miniseries from USA TODAY bestselling author Carol Marinelli

Siblings Sebastián, Alejandro and Carmen Romero are heirs to a renowned sherry empire in Spain. To the world, they have it all: charm, status and wealth. But their parents' stormy marriage has also left the siblings with a legacy of emotional wariness, which has meant the empire always came before love. Now, is that all about to change?

Read Alejandro's story in
His Innocent for One Spanish Night

Read Sebastián's story in
Midnight Surrender to the Spaniard

And look out for Carmen's story, coming soon!

Carol Marinelli

—

MIDNIGHT SURRENDER
TO THE SPANIARD

HARLEQUIN
PRESENTS

HARLEQUIN®
PRESENTS™

ISBN-13: 978-1-335-58450-2

Midnight Surrender to the Spaniard

Copyright © 2023 by Carol Marinelli

Recycling programs
for this product may
not exist in your area.

For questions and comments about the quality of this book,
please contact us at CustomerService@Harlequin.com.

Harlequin Enterprises ULC
22 Adelaide St. West, 41st Floor
Toronto, Ontario M5H 4E3, Canada
www.Harlequin.com

Printed in U.S.A.

Carol Marinelli recently filled in a form asking for her job title. Thrilled to be able to put down her answer, she put "writer." Then it asked what Carol did for relaxation and she put down the truth—"writing." The third question asked for her hobbies. Well, not wanting to look obsessed, she crossed her fingers and answered "swimming"—but, given that the chlorine in the pool does terrible things to her highlights, I'm sure you can guess the real answer!

CHAPTER ONE

'MARRIED?'

At first Anna Douglas thought her friend was joking. After all, you couldn't read facial expressions in a phone call, and Emily had only been in Spain for six weeks.

'Anna, I know it's fast, but I want one person at least to be happy for us...'

The smile on Anna's face faded as she heard the slight desperation in her friend's tone.

'His whole family are against it. Sebastián thinks I'm some sort of gold-digger...'

'What?'

'Oh, yes. While Alejandro was in the States, Sebastián fired me and terminated my accommodation at the bodega in an attempt to break us up. He practically threw me out...'

'Sebastián?'

Anna frowned, because he was one of the Romero brothers. She'd heard that name a few times in recent weeks. Emily had been working on the website of some luxurious sherry bodega, and from everything Anna had gleaned he didn't sound in the least pleasant.

'Hold on a moment. Just who are you marrying?'

'Alejandro,' Emily said, and Anna's heart sank when she realised her shy friend was actually involved with one of the Romero brothers.

They were billionaire playboys with dreadful reputations. Anna only knew this because she'd read up on them when her friend had taken the role.

It got worse.

The wedding was to take place in two weeks' time and, yes, her friend confided, she was pregnant…

'We're only telling his parents.'

Anna, a little bolder and rather more forthright than her friend, had been about to advise her to slow things down, but when she heard about the pregnancy she closed both her lips and her eyes.

'Anna, I need your support on this.'

'You *always* have my support.'

Unequivocally.

After all, Emily was the only one in the entire village who had stood by her during the darkest of times.

It was quite a long phone call, filled with a mixture of tears and excitement from Emily as Anna did her best to remain calm and sound upbeat about this sudden May wedding!

'Please say you and Willow will be there.'

'The thing is…' Anna halted, not sure what to say to her dearest friend.

For once it wasn't about money, because Emily had told her that Alejandro was insisting on paying for their flights and accommodation. The issue was that Willow had had a string of painful ear infections and was waiting for minor surgery.

'Anna, please. You have to be there.'

It was a relief when the call ended. Anna sat on the sofa and, resting her elbows on her knees, scrunched her fists around handfuls of her long blonde hair and let out a tense breath.

Do something, Anna!

She was soon on the computer, on the very website her best friend had designed, reading about the groom, his brother, and their younger sister Carmen—who, Emily had told her, had also done her best to break up the couple.

Her eyes met those of Sebastián Romero—the eldest of the siblings and the one most opposed to the marriage. He was leaning against a wall, or a balcony, high up on a roof terrace, and smiling into the camera. Anna ignored his dark good looks and suave appearance. Instead she noticed that his smile didn't reach his black eyes…

He looked a formidable opponent indeed.

'Oh, Emily…' she groaned.

Anna made her way up the stairs and quietly pushed open the bedroom door to see her daughter asleep on top of the bed, with all her soft toys tucked up inside it.

Gently, trying not to wake her, Anna put Willow in with the toys, tucking them all in, and then sat on the edge of the bed for a moment and looked at the bottle of eardrops on the bedside table.

Of course Anna wanted to be there to support her friend, but she knew that the changes in pressure caused by flying would likely cause her daughter pain. Until she had the surgery it was out of the question for Willow to fly. Yet Emily had been there for Anna every step of the way—even if Anna hadn't quite told her everything about Willow's father...

She hadn't been able to tell anyone. She had clammed up so badly when she'd tried to tell her parents that they'd wrongly concluded that their daughter had fallen pregnant after some nameless one-night stand.

Four, almost five years later, her relationship with them was still incredibly strained. They adored Willow, though, determinedly not blaming the child for the sins of the mother...

It was to be Anna's second difficult phone call of the night: explaining to her mother that Emily had invited her and Willow to her wedding in Spain in just a fortnight...

'What about Willow's ears?' Jean Douglas immediately pointed out. 'Do you really think she should be flying?'

'No, I don't,' Anna admitted. 'That's why I'm calling you. I was wondering if you'd be able to look after her for the weekend. I'd fly out on the Friday and be back on Sunday.'

She listened to the long stretch of silence that followed. Anna's mother had the same pale green eyes as her, and though Anna could just picture them, rolling at her daughter's audacity, she pushed her request.

'You did say that you wanted to be more involved with Willow.'

'And what if we can't look after her?' her mother said. 'It's Ascension Day, and—'

'I know that,' Anna broke in. Because of course she knew that the fortieth day of Easter—Ascension Day—would fall on that Sunday. Her father was the parish vicar, and their lives ran on church time. 'If you can't have her, then I completely understand.'

'What would you do?'

'I don't know,' Anna admitted. 'I'll speak to her GP and see if there's...' She swallowed.

It would be a two-hour flight from London to Seville, followed by a train journey to Jerez, and Willow, with her adventurous spirit, would be thrilled to go.

She asked herself the very question her mother had.

What *would* she do if her mother said she couldn't have Willow?

'If you can't take her then I won't go,' Anna said, though it tore her apart to say so. Emily had been there for her all her life—more than her blood family in recent years. Yet Willow had to come first. 'There's no one else I'd consider leaving her with.'

Even though her parents' reaction to her pregnancy had broken her own heart, she trusted them with Willow's. Willow saw her grandparents at church, and for birthdays and such, and loved them dearly. She adored spending time with them and was always pleading for a sleepover.

Her parents had so far refused.

They'd told Anna, even before she'd given birth, that they would not be used as a babysitting service.

'Very well.' She could hear her mother choking on her magnanimous words. 'We'll have Willow for the weekend.'

And even though she thanked her mother profusely, in truth she'd almost wanted her to say no.

Anna hadn't had a single night apart from Willow since she was born, and two nights felt by far too many.

CHAPTER TWO

THERE WOULD BE no train journey to Jerez.

Anna had been told that Sebastián Romero would be waiting to greet her at Seville Airport.

Apparently it was a tradition that the *padrino*—the Spanish equivalent of a best man—took care of such details on the eve of the wedding.

Anna had been warned about him, so she had read up on him some more.

It had never entered Anna's head that she might like him.

She wore a loose skirt and halter-neck top with flat sandals—a pretty non-descript outfit—and so on stepping into Arrivals she expected to have to cast her eyes around to find a guy holding up a sign with her name or…

Yet straight away her eyes locked with his.

He was tall, and wore a suit and loosened tie. He looked bored, brooding, and although she was both shocked and loath to admit it, he was beautiful.

He gave her a nod, and as she wheeled her case around and walked towards him, he gave her a sort of half-smile.

Well, a quarter of a smile.

'Sebastián…' She didn't know if she should offer her hand, nor quite how to greet this reluctant *padrino*.

'Sebastián?' he frowned. 'No.'

Realising she'd been mistaken, Anna backed away. 'Oh, gosh, sorry…'

'*Es broma…*' he said. 'Joking.'

Anna was surprised by her own smile.

'Is there a problem with your luggage?' He glanced at her small case. 'Has it not come through?'

'No, I've just got carry-on. I'm only here for two nights.'

'One of them *is* a wedding,' he said.

Anna took that as a criticism.

He must have seen her lips pinch. 'I meant that is the size of a make-up bag for most women…' He rolled his beautiful black eyes as if he knew he'd possibly offended her again. 'Let's get to the car.'

Surprisingly, she wasn't offended.

Anna was actually somewhat startled by the ease of her smile at his little joke about not being Sebastián when just moments before, as she'd exited the plane, she'd called the vicarage and spoken on the phone to an excited Willow. The conversation had left her fighting tears.

'Nanny and I are making scones!'

'How lovely.'

'Give Em a kiss for me.'

'I shall.'

'Send lots of pictures too.'

Anna had felt too far away from her daughter, and tearful that it had taken nearly five years for this to happen.

Yet Willow had sounded completely happy, and so she'd blinked away the tears. Moments later, when she'd been met by Sebastián and his dry humour, Anna had found herself smiling.

Despite the joke, it was clear he did not want to be here. She didn't take it personally, and knew it was because he was vehemently opposed to the wedding. He was scrupulously polite, despite his feelings about his brother's decision to marry Anna's friend.

As they left the airport, stepping out into the gorgeous May sun, Anna got her first glimpse of Emily's new world.

'Anna!' Sebastián called her back.

It was then that she realised they were *not* walking with the masses to the car park.

A low silver car was mere steps away, and Anna saw a valet hand Sebastián his keys before stowing her carry-on bag in the boot.

'So,' Sebastián said as he manoeuvred the car out on to the main road, 'it's about an hour to Jerez. I'm to drop you at the bridal boutique and then I'll take your case to the hotel.'

'I can manage my own case.'

'You are the *dama de honor*. It is expected.'

Those last words told her everything she needed to know about his attitude towards his reluctant duty.

'How was your flight?' he enquired politely.

'Fine, thank you.'

'There was a wedding rehearsal last night…'

'I know. I couldn't get away sooner.'

Her throat went tight at the thought of Willow, so far away, and, not wanting to start crying, she hurriedly looked out of the window rather than mention her daughter.

Aside from the threat of tears, she doubted this sophisticated man would be remotely interested in her babysitting arrangements.

They drove in silence for most of the way, but as they approached Jerez he leant over, and she felt his arm brush her thigh. She was startled, but it turned out he was just opening up the glove box and taking out an envelope.

It was for her.

'That's your hotel card. It is close to the church.'

He explained the details and she tried not to blush, but found she was just so *aware* of how she had reacted to the brief contact.

'Whatever you may have heard about me, I'm not *that* bad…'

Anna frowned, and then realised he was addressing her overreaction when he'd reached over.

When it registered, she laughed. 'Sorry, I just—'

'It's okay.'

He glanced over again and gave her a smile.

Definitely a half-smile this time.

Or at least more than a quarter.

'You didn't miss much at the rehearsal,' he said,

turning his eyes back to the road. 'You are to stay with the bride and walk in with her.'

'Behind her?'

'I don't know,' he admitted. 'I wasn't taking notes.'

'You must know what usually happens at a Spanish wedding.'

'We don't usually have bridesmaids.' He shrugged. 'You'll be fine. Just make sure the bride and groom don't come in contact tomorrow until the church. You and Emily are both staying in the hotel. I am too...'

'Is that where the function's being held?' Anna asked.

'No, apart from the service, everything is taking place in the bodega.'

'Oh.'

She knew that Alejandro had a residence in the bodega, and had assumed Sebastián must too, but he said nothing to further enlighten her.

'I'll call you when we get to the church and then you'll walk the bride over...'

'Walk her over?' Anna checked. 'In brand-new shoes I've never even seen, let alone tried on?'

'You can blame your friend for that. Emily wanted a very quick wedding.' He stared pointedly ahead. 'I wonder why that is?'

His words dripped sarcasm but Anna said nothing. She knew he was testing her reaction and refused to give him one.

Instead she carried on gazing out of the window as they drove through Jerez. Emily had not over-stated its beauty and Anna was enjoying the view.

Sebastián wasn't much of a tourist guide, though he did comment when they passed the esteemed equestrian school where the famous dancing horses performed.

'My sister Carmen practically lives there.'

Apart from that he left it to Anna to take in the Moorish buildings on her own. The stunning Al-cázar with its ancient baths looked incredible, and there were beautiful plazas with fountains and tiny streets she would have loved to explore.

'It's a shame I'm only here for two days.'

He gave a slight mirthless laugh. 'I'm sure you'll be back to visit your friend.'

He didn't say *your newly rich friend*, but she knew she was meant to infer that.

As he pulled the car to a halt, Anna realised they were outside the bridal boutique. She decided his words merited a response.

'Oh, I shall certainly be back, Sebastián.' Her eyes met his, and now that the car had stopped he fully met her gaze. 'Emily is more than a friend. I consider her to be my sister, so I'll definitely be visiting in the future.'

Anna had been determined to remain smiling and polite throughout the proceedings, but had nev-ertheless felt every barb about Emily. Now that she'd realised something of what her friend was up against, she decided she would speak up.

'You're not the only one who has concerns about the suddenness of this wedding.'

He gave the slightest of sardonic smiles, clearly not believing her for a moment, so Anna let him know that she'd done her research on the man who would marry her friend.

'Your brother doesn't exactly come with the best references, and as for—'

She stopped herself then, but knew there was a flush spreading across her neck and cheeks. Because taking the groom's *brother* to task for his sexual history was not part of a bridesmaid's or a best friend's job description. Though it had gone unsaid, Anna rather guessed she'd revealed that she'd done her homework on him...

Oh, indeed, she had.

And if she'd thought Alejandro was bad... Sebastián was wicked.

It wasn't just stories of the wild parties aboard his yacht that had shocked Anna and kept her reading late into the night, but the stream of tearful women who had tried to love him.

The *endless* stream!

There was even a devastated ex-fiancée, whom he'd allegedly broken up with a couple of weeks after she'd lost their baby. All the scurrilous gossip sites managed to get the word *allegedly* in, presumably for legal reasons, and yet he'd done nothing that Anna could see to dispel the widespread rumours.

Even though she hadn't voiced any of this to Sebastián, Anna wondered if she'd gone too far.

Not that it seemed to bother him. He barely blinked—just coolly held her gaze.

Flustered suddenly, she looked down a little, but only got as far as his mouth.

It was *such* an exquisite mouth. His lips were full and the cupid's bow so defined that not even an hour with a lip liner brush could have made it better.

'Finished?' he checked, and Anna realised her eyes were still on his full mouth.

So, no, she had not finished looking. His white front teeth had met his bottom lip as he'd pronounced the *F* and then his teeth had pressed together on the *D*, and then his lips had stayed slightly parted…

She dragged her eyes back to his.

'Finished.'

She attempted a firm response but heard the tremble in her voice as she said it. She turned her head to the front window. Why had she said that? Why had she been about to allude to his reputation when it had less than nothing to do with her?

'Let's just get through tomorrow,' he suggested, although there was an edge to his voice that told her he wasn't best pleased. *'Hasta luego,'* he added.

She blinked, wondering if she'd just been insulted.

'It means *goodbye*,' he translated. 'Or rather, *until later*.'

Until later!

Sebastián did not help her with her luggage. He was through with being polite and pointedly just popped open the boot, remaining in the driver's seat.

There was fire beneath that rather icy exterior, he thought. Reluctantly, he admired her for standing up for her friend, and for facing him as she told him what she thought of Alejandro and this sudden wedding. But then she had alluded to his own behaviour… He had thought himself numb to those accusations. After all, he knew the truth. Yet her green kitten eyes had felt like a flashlight, aimed directly at him.

For a second he had actually considered tartly suggesting that she should not believe everything she read…

No.

He would not be explaining himself and he did not care what anyone else thought, Sebastián reminded himself, watching her wheel her case towards the boutique.

This *dama de honor* also had a very beautiful back…pale and straight. He had noticed it at the airport as she'd walked ahead to the car, her slender frame accentuating the winged scapula.

Watching her walk to the boutique now, he found the pale blonde ponytail a mild irritant—but only because it concealed her graceful spine.

Perhaps she'd felt his stare, because he saw she'd stiffened briefly and halted as she arrived at the door of the boutique.

And then he further admired her, because she turned and faced him again. For a moment contempt was written on her features, but then she smiled a wide smile, turned away, and went in to greet her friend.

Unseen, Sebastián smiled too. His smile was surprisingly genuine, even though he knew Anna's was fixed in place for her friend—which let him know she was going along with this damned wedding just as reluctantly as he…

Indeed, Anna had fixed on her smile for Emily's benefit, and while she was thrilled to see her friend, she really was concerned.

'Anna!' Emily hugged her fiercely. 'I am so sorry to have inflicted Sebastián on you.'

'He was fine.'

'Please!' Emily was disbelieving. 'If I hadn't had to get my dress let out I'd have been there to greet you and to hell with tradition. Come and see it.'

Her friend was ecstatic, Anna realised. Glowing…

'And come and try yours on. If you don't like it then there are others.'

'I love it,' Anna said—and she did. It was made of heavy silk in a very deep amber colour, and possibly—probably—the most beautiful item of clothing she'd ever held, let alone tried on.

The dressmaker gestured for her to put a scarf over her head and face.

'The dress goes on over your head,' Emily said, smiling at Anna's bemused expression. 'The scarf's so you don't get any make-up on it.'

'I'm not wearing any.'

But still, she complied, and the dark silk slid over her head and down her body. As the dressmaker did the zip up Anna held her breath—and not because the dress was tight…

It was definitely the most beautiful thing she'd ever worn.

'You look stunning, Anna!' Emily beamed. 'I haven't seen you all dressed up in…'

She didn't finish.

Even Anna couldn't remember when.

Her last night out had been a Christmas function with the staff from the school where she worked as a part-time receptionist, and it had hardly been dressy.

And the time before that…

Rather than dwell on her lack of social life, Anna tried on the shoes her friend had chosen. They were neutral, but strappy and high—especially given Anna didn't usually wear heels.

'I hope I don't trip…'

In the end, it was a day of much pampering. The hotel was elegant, with uniformed doormen and bellboys, and there was even a lift man who pulled back the ancient iron gated doors of the elevator and did the same again when you reached your floor.

Her suite overlooked the beautiful Plaza de Santiago. Anna looked down at the square and to the fountain, then across to the church where the wedding going to be held. It looked more like a cathedral, she thought.

'Are there are a lot of guests coming?'

'Hundreds.' Emily nodded. 'And half of them are Alejandro's exes—or at least it feels that way. Mariana's coming…'

'The one he was supposed to marry?'

'According to his father and brother,' Emily said. 'Apparently they wanted to merge the bodegas. I think that's why Sebastián's so angry. He only cares about the business.'

'Emily…' Anna took a breath. They were finally face to face and alone and it had to be said. 'I'm only going to say this once—'

'Please don't.'

They had been friends long enough that Emily had guessed what she was about to say.

'We're not just marrying because of the baby. Anna, I've seen how marvellously you've done on your own…'

'Hardly marvellously!'

'You've done it though—all by yourself. If Alejandro and I weren't in love then I'd go it alone. You've shown me how!'

'Okay… Well, it looks like we've got a wedding to get to tomorrow.'

After Emily's reassurances, Anna wished she could simply relax and enjoy it, but even as they sat at the elegant hotel restaurant she felt unusually flustered.

She was missing Willow, Anna told herself as they ate paella. But she'd just called her daughter, and everything at home was fine. So was it just that she felt out of place in such luxurious surroundings? Especially as she so rarely went out?

No, it wasn't that, Anna acknowledged to herself. She was by far too aware that Sebastián was staying in the same hotel.

'Why is Sebastián staying here?' Anna asked. 'I thought there were residences on their property.'

'They have places all over,' Emily said. 'It's only Alejandro who lives at the bodega. Sebastián goes there just for work, thank goodness. I'd hate to be his neighbour.'

'What about the rest of the family? Are they *all* against the wedding? You said Alejandro's father was coming round?'

'José's starting to—but only because of the baby. Carmen actively dislikes me. Incredibly, the only one who seems remotely supportive is Maria, their mother.'

'She's the famous flamenco dancer?' Anna checked. 'Why is it incredible that's she's supportive?'

'Because apparently she's the coldest fish of the lot.'

Later, as they left the restaurant, Anna found out she had been right to be on high alert—because she came face to face again with Sebastián. He was talking to the concierge, but when he caught sight of them he turned and called for them to wait.

Goodness, he was so commanding, Anna thought as he walked confidently towards him.

'Everything is organised,' he informed Emily. 'Is there anything else you need?'

'We're fine, thank you, Sebastián,' Emily replied.

And then his black eyes moved to Anna.

'Our most important role before the wedding is to ensure the bride and groom do not see each other prior to the church.'

'Yes.' She gave a tight smile. 'It's the same in England. We—'

He cut her off, clearly not willing to make idle conversation. 'I'll call you when we have arrived at the church.'

'Okay.'

'So I will need your number.'

Call Emily, she wanted to say. But of course she did not want him to see how much he rattled her. It was clear they would have to correspond on the big day, so she gave him her number and watched as he typed it in.

'Thank you,' he said, and then turned his stern attention back to Emily. 'Best wishes for tomorrow.'

He stalked off—though not in the direction of the elevators, nor the exit. Instead he walked down a long stone corridor towards a huge intricately carved arched wooden door.

'Best wishes, indeed,' Emily muttered sarcastically.

Anna found she was still watching him. She saw him take out a key and open the door, through which she glimpsed a courtyard. She had to mentally shake herself to force her attention away.

'Let's head up,' she said to the bride-to-be. 'You've got a big day tomorrow.'

So did Anna.

Her nails and make-up had been professionally done, and her hair cut, blow-dried and smoothed until it was as silky as the dress she slid on.

Now there was nothing left to do other than make the promised video call to Willow.

'Mummy!' She was so excited. 'You look lovely!'

'So do you, darling.'

Anna smiled, because Willow had dressed for the occasion and was wearing the flamenco dress that Emily had bought for her.

'I wanted to wear lipstick...' Willow's voice dropped to a whisper. 'But Nanny doesn't have *any*!'

'You look beautiful without. Now, are you ready to see how gorgeous Emily looks in her dress?'

CHAPTER THREE

'*SE VE HERMOSA*...' *She looks beautiful*...

As the bride entered the magnificent church Sebastián Romero gritted his jaw, yet he turned and looked down the aisle, ready to force a smile, willing to do his duty as his brother's *padrino* and murmur appropriate words to his brother and all the guests.

Just for today.

Of *course* the bride would be looking beautiful—who wouldn't be glowing and smiling when they'd guaranteed themselves a meal ticket for life?

He was certain Emily was pregnant—and, no, he did not believe it was possible to fall in love and decide you wanted a baby all in a matter of weeks.

He knew from bitter experience.

And Sebastián's hardened, cynical nature wasn't reserved for the bride.

He glanced over to his parents. His father, four weeks out of surgery, was determinedly standing. As for Maria—who did not deserve the title of 'mother'—for the first time in twenty-five years she was by her husband's side.

Sebastián had no doubt her return was down to the fact that José Romero was dying. The ink on his newly written will was barely dry and Sebastián was certain it would be in Maria's favour...

Hell, yes, he was jaded and bitter—unlike Alejandro, who had stars in his eyes. English stars! The woman they had hired to revamp the Romero website had revamped much more than they had intended.

He looked back to the bride, resigned to saying the right thing—only his black gaze didn't make it that far. Instead it fell on her *dama de honor.*

Anna.

Her long blonde hair was straight and worn down, held back from her face with a couple of sprigs of orange blossom.

The dress was elegant and a deep amber—almost the colour of the sherry the Romeros produced. Certainly the silk was just as fluid as it skimmed her slender body. The spaghetti straps showed her clavicles, and his eyes moved up her long neck to her face.

'*Sí, se ve hermosa,*' Sebastián finally said to his brother. *Yes, she looks beautiful.*

Sebastián had said the appropriate words to Alejandro—and with conviction.

Only he wasn't referring to the bride…

Closer now, he saw Anna's made-up eyes and mouth and noticed that her pale cheeks were rouged—or perhaps she blushed a little as she met his gaze. He nodded to her—an acknowledgement, thanking her for delivering the bride—then turned away.

He was actually a touch disconcerted by the force of his attraction towards Anna.

Although, he thought, on reflection, he appreciated the distraction on this hellish day.

The priest spoke of love eternal and again he tightened his jaw unconsciously. He took a deep breath and tried to decide if he preferred Anna with makeup or without. He might kiss that lipstick off later...

Now he was being asked for the rings...

Sebastián wished he could toss them away.

Truly.

He was tempted to fling the rings into the congregation to register his protest.

Not for a second did he believe that this was a love match.

Not for a second did he believe in love.

Even when he'd been engaged himself it had been about duty, about doing the right thing...

His mouth pressed together.

Had there been love?

Not for Ella, who had briefly been his fiancée.

For the baby?

A baby that hadn't even existed...

One was crying in the church now. Loudly. Then another baby joined in, and then another... In this sacred space their screams felt like a mockery, a pertinent reminder that it had taken a lie about a baby for him to even consider becoming a husband.

Never.

Anna's doubts were fading.

She didn't doubt her friend was in love, and the

way Alejandro smiled at Emily and recited his vows told Anna it wasn't as one-sided as she'd feared.

It looked like love—not that Anna had much to go on when it came to judging.

Had she just been jealous? Or was she right to have been worried by this whirlwind romance?

Here she was, standing in a gorgeous old church, watching her best friend get married. Her eyes came to rest on Sebastián. He was looking fixedly ahead, allowing Anna a quiet moment to observe his serious beauty.

It felt odd to register attraction.

To notice how his perfectly cut suit adorned broad shoulders and to try not to wonder whether or not they would dance later.

Odd to be so fascinated by the back of his head and to notice that his hair had been trimmed since yesterday, those thick black strands growing into a V at the back of his olive-skinned neck.

Just bizarre to stand in a church in front of two hundred or so people and for the first time in years feel her heart trip like a schoolgirl's.

Or, to blush like a naïve university student when a good-looking visiting professor smiled.

She quashed down that memory and got back to focussing on Sebastián.

No, it didn't just feel odd to be so drawn to an-other—it felt unfamiliar and new. Anna had never been so violently attracted to anyone.

But this was a physical reaction.

Purely physical.

Because, from everything she'd seen and heard so far, she didn't like Sebastián Romero very much at all.

Yet her lips betrayed her…because they seemed to smile or laugh at his bidding.

And her heart seemed detached from her logical mind whenever he was near and it beat more rapidly.

She watched as he was prompted to hand over the rings.

He reached into the pocket of his immaculate dark suit. Was it just her or was there a slight hesitation as he held them over the bible and then dropped them onto the pages? Anna found that her lips were attempting to betray her again, because she had to pinch an incoming smile at his truculence. He continued his vigil, staring fixedly ahead, but as the vows were exchanged and the babies started wailing again he arched his tense neck and looked up at the magnificent roof.

He was, Anna knew, hating every second of this.

Still, he was supremely polite when they went through to the vestry for the signings.

'Did I mess up the vows?' Emily asked.

She had made hers in Spanish, and Alejandro had given his in English.

'You were wonderful,' Anna said, smiling. 'Not that I speak Spanish, but it all—'

'Ladies,' Sebastián interrupted, 'the photographer wants a picture of the four of us with the priest.'

'Of course,' Emily said, and made her way over to the large table and took a seat as the photographer said something in Spanish to Anna.

She didn't understand. 'I'm sorry?' she said.

'He wants you to stand behind the bride,' Sebastián translated. 'Next to me.'

'Okay.' She took her place by his side and felt a frisson of awareness, as if the heat from her body had met the heat from his, even though they stood apart from each other.

Sebastián took her arm to guide her closer.

Don't react, she told herself. *You shouldn't even notice.*

The photographer was moving them like chess pieces, but Sebastián's light touch had her fizzing with awareness.

'Más cerca,' the photographer said, waving his hands at them.

'We are to move closer.' Sebastián translated again. 'And we are to remember to smile.'

'He didn't say all that.'

'He said one of those things,' Sebastián responded—and Anna found that she did both: she moved closer *and* she smiled.

And then it was all over and they made their way to the reception. The bodega was incredible, and every bit as beautiful as Emily had described. What they called the cellar was in fact a huge church-like area supported by arches and filled with black barrels of the Romero sherry. There were round stained-glass windows and a stage at one end of the room. Anna knew it was also used as a restaurant, and there was a *taberna* too, which Emily whisked her off to see.

'This is where we met.'

'I've never seen anything like it,' Anna said as she stared at walls lined with photos of flamenco dancing.

Staff were passing around trays of coffee and sherry. It was the perfect opportunity for guests to catch their breath. Anna had been told the wedding would go on deep into the night.

Emily was soon called away and Anna found herself back in the courtyard, helping herself to some food at a delicious-looking spread of tapas.

'Take it slow…'

Even before she heard his voice, Anna knew it was *him*.

'Believe me, there is more to come.'

'Oh!' She looked down at her rather full plate. 'I thought this was dinner.'

'Oh, no,' he said, taking one of her pastries. 'For now it is just food while there is talking. Later we have a sit-down dinner, and that goes on for hours.'

'Do you have your speech ready?' Anna asked.

'No speeches.'

'Pity…' Anna started, and then bit down on the remaining words, for she'd been about to say that she'd been looking forward to finding out more about him. She never flirted. *Ever.* She did not even know how. And yet she realised she had been about to with him.

'Are you okay?' he asked.

'Of course.'

'I'm aware you don't know anyone here. Just call out if you need a translator or anything.'

Anna knew he was just being polite. 'I'll be fine.'

But then he surprised her: 'Do you want a quick rundown?'

'Sorry?'

'If you're going to be people-watching?' He looked out at the other guests. 'Right...see the woman in silver with the *peineta*?'

'Yes.'

'That's Maria—our mother. With her stands my devoted father, José. See the young lady with black hair?'

'There are a lot of ladies with black hair,' Anna pointed out.

'Her dress is bronze and she's sulking and drinking champagne. That's Carmen—my sister.'

'Okay...' Anna was reluctantly touched that he would take the time to make being on her own at the wedding a little more fun.

'That one...' He'd turned his back to the crowd now and was talking directly to her. 'Don't make it obvious you're looking,' he warned. 'She has shorter black hair and her dress is...' He hesitated. 'I don't know the English for that word.' He thought for a moment. 'She looks as if she is sucking lemons…'

'In pink?'

'I know *that* word.' He shot out a laugh. 'Ugly pink.'

'That's not nice.'

'It's an actual shade,' he informed her. 'Anyway, that is Mariana!'

'Ooh!' Anna was intrigued that he had pointed out the main characters in Alejandro and Emily's whirlwind love story, but soon he was being called away.

'I have to go now.' He took another pastry from her plate. 'I'll come and get you when it's our turn to dance.'

He was so arrogant, clearing her plate when there was a full tapas bar behind him, but as it turned out she ended up being rather grateful, because the evening meal was huge.

Huge and long.

She was seated with Emily on one side of her and—with only Anna to represent Emily's family, perhaps to add balance to the table—on the other side, the very sulky Carmen.

Anna attempted conversation. 'I passed the equestrian centre yesterday.'

Carmen barely looked up.

'I hear you like horse riding?'

'I would hope so, given that it's my profession.'

Anna gave up trying to get blood from a stone, and was grateful when the meal seemed to be over. But then, just when she thought it was finished, a team of waiters filed out, carrying more plates above their shoulders.

For a brief second, and actually by accident, she caught Sebastián's eye and he smiled and mouthed, *Told you*.

Again her lips betrayed her and she smiled.

And so to the dancing...

Anna had not been looking forward to it. In fact, she'd been dreading it a little. But not any more. For now she found she was tense with anticipation.

As she watched the bride and groom dancing together, out of the corner of her eye she saw Sebastián approach. He stopped by her chair and offered his hand.

'Anna?'

'Thank you.'

She took his hand and stood, and of course then he released her, but that brief touch of his cool skin was their first real contact.

How could his hands be so cold on this hot night? She already knew he did not have a warm heart, but his fingers were like ice!

He reclaimed her hand again when they were on the dance floor and his other hand lightly held her waist. It was all very formal and polite—but the conversation, on the other hand, was not.

'It's a lovely wedding,' Anna said.

'Oh, please. Don't tell me you're a believer now?'

'They seem happy.'

'Even those babies registered their protest,' he said as they twirled and spun about the floor.

She thought of him arching his neck in the church—looking heavenwards for the strength to endure it, perhaps.

'My father lets children run up and down the aisles during the service,' she said, then added, 'He's a vicar.'

'Oh.' He thought for a moment and looked around. 'Then he would love a Spanish wedding. There's no such thing as bedtime here. Unfortunately!'

'You don't think children should be allowed at the reception?' Anna asked, and thought of Willow who, if she were here, would be dashing around and making friends, as well as a whole lot of noise. 'I think it's lovely.'

'Then welcome to Jerez,' he said dryly, and gave a small laugh. 'I am the…' His voice paused, perhaps in order to select the correct word, but his body kept moving, lithe and strong. He never missed a beat and carried on smoothly, turning and guiding her through the steps. Then his voice came deep in her ear—deep and close. 'I am the killjoy.'

Anna said nothing, but as another couple moved a little too near she was momentarily grateful that he pulled her in close. Then it dawned on her that her face was on his chest, and she felt less relieved.

He never stopped moving—just effortlessly corrected their position and shielded them from the rather more flamboyant displays on the dance floor. Despite being on show, in front of two hundred people, she felt hidden—as if he'd taken her into an alternative world for two where they shared private thoughts and conversation.

'Maybe I am too cynical...' Now he did pause, that effortless grace momentarily suspended, as if he were deep in thought. 'I just question people's motives...'

'Not everyone has a motive, Sebastián. Some people are just...' Anna hesitated. She didn't want to call her best friend naïve on her wedding day, even if that was what she privately thought.

'Some people are...?' he queried, prompting her to go on.

But Anna had lost her train of thought.

The music had slowed and she wished the dance would end.

Not because of the discomfort.

More because of the awareness.

She was a young woman—a mother—so clearly not naïve, and yet that was exactly the word she would have chosen for herself now, if asked.

Naïve because she had never known how alive her body could feel.

Naïve because she'd thought she'd known what attraction felt like, and yet what she had felt before was pale and drab in comparison to what she was experiencing now.

'Some people…?' he said, prompting her again.

She lifted her head and looked into his black eyes for a moment before answering.

'Are too trusting,' Anna said.

'You are not?'

'Oh, no.' She shook her head. *Not any more.* 'But you're wrong about Emily.'

'I hope so.'

'They're clearly in love.'

'Please!' He gave a mocking laugh, but then conceded a touch. 'Well, if it's the love match of the century then good luck to them. *I* wouldn't want it.'

'You don't want love?' Anna frowned.

'God, no. Another damn person to worry about? No, thank you.'

She laughed—actually laughed—understanding a little what he meant. Because since Willow had been born she'd felt as if she was walking around with her heart in her mouth. Then she heard her own laughter and it sounded so carefree…a sound she had forgotten—almost foreign. Perhaps it was the sound of *Spanish* laughter!

But the moment was short-lived, for the music had ended. The dance she had both anticipated and dreaded was over, and she found herself wishing that he might not notice…that their dance would go on…

Instead, duty done, he thanked her and let her go.

It was possibly just as well, because there was stamping from those on the stage, and shouts of *'Olé!'* from the guests, and the tempo of the music picked up in response.

Anna was ill equipped for any of that.

'I must go and do my best man duty and dance with my mother...'

'Is it a tradition?' Anna asked.

'No...' He shrugged. 'But it is necessary if she is to be prevented from making this *her* night. She loves the spotlight. If I don't stop her it will become the Maria de Luca show.'

'Olé!'

'Olé!'

'Olé!'

Gosh, thought Anna, the Spanish really danced! Emily was showing off the results of her flamenco lessons as Alejandro encouraged her. Maria had started stamping her feet, clearly having fun. Even José got up—to the delight of everyone. And Sebastián could stamp his boots with the best of them.

Only the sulking Carmen remained seated.

Anna danced with a couple of other guests, but found her eyes kept drifting towards Sebastián. He had a cigar in his mouth, and although she *hated* smoking, it seemed that was what all Spanish guys did at a wedding. His hands were above his head and he was clapping and stamping and very possibly the sexiest man alive.

Oh, my!

Willow would have loved this, Anna thought, when her dance with a man who wasn't Sebastián ended. She decided now might be the right time to slip outside and call her daughter.

'Do you miss me?' Willow asked.

'Very much,' Anna said, looking at the black barrels piled high in the vast Romero bodega and the stained-glass windows above. Then she noticed a young couple kissing in the shadows, and turned her back.

She envied them, Anna realised as she ended her call with Willow after telling her to be a good girl for Nanny and Grandpa and… 'go to bed when they tell you. Sweet dreams…'

Her attention returned to the couple in the shadows. Dancing the night away and then sneaking off for a kiss…

It was romantic—all the things a perfect night should be—and something she had never properly known herself…

She didn't even like kissing, Anna reminded herself with a little shake.

Heading back to the table, she felt betwixt and between not just two worlds—her life in England and this glamorous night in Spain—but another life too…one she had been on the threshold of…

During her third year at university she'd hoped to join in more, have fun, loosen up a touch. While her friends had all considered her to be forthright and bold, when it came to intimacy, Anna hadn't been.

Anna had hidden.

She'd always dressed conservatively—the judgemental sniffs from her mother at her clothes not worth the effort of rebelling. And she'd always had the eyes of the entire congregation upon her in the village.

University had been overwhelming, and she'd focussed on studying rather than revelling in her new freedoms. Then, in her final year, she'd met someone—or rather had been flattered by the rare attention he had bestowed upon her.

But despite enjoying the attention, kissing and touching—*anything* physical—had had to be coaxed out of her. She'd kept on waiting to enjoy it, and until now she'd assumed it was guilt that had held her back, or that she just wasn't a particularly sexual person.

She took her seat at the almost empty head table, grateful not to be the only one. Carmen was still sitting everything out—though she did at least acknowledge Anna's presence.

'God, I wish this was over.' Carmen pouted and then glanced up and rolled her eyes as Sebastián came over and said something scathing in Spanish.

He took a seat beside Anna, because Carmen was at the end of the table and he had no choice but to do so. He at least had the grace to apologise before talking across Anna in Spanish.

'Carmen...' Whatever he said to his sister in

rapid Spanish caused her to flash Sebastián an angry look.

'No!' she said angrily, and they argued on.

Possibly because their father had come to sit at the table they switched to English, perhaps not wanting him to understand, and Anna, who wasn't generally a nosy person—well, perhaps just a bit—felt as if her ears were on elastic as she eavesdropped unashamedly.

'Carmen, talk to your father,' Sebastián told her.

'He's making a fool of himself.'

Anna realised then that they were speaking about José, who sat watching his wife dance, surrounded by male admirers. As Sebastián had predicted, Maria was making the night all about herself. Anna wondered if they were all being just a little harsh in their judgement, but she knew she did not know the full history.

Not that Emily and Alejandro seemed to mind… They were locked together, swaying with the music.

'Tonight is Papá's dream,' Sebastián said.

'No, he wanted Alejandro to marry Mariana.'

'Well, tonight romance wins,' Sebastián said with a wry edge. 'Carmen…' His voice was low. 'He's sick. God knows, there might never be another night like this when we're all together at a celebration.'

'Sebastián, por favor no digas eso.'

The desperation and expression in Carmen's voice meant that Anna, even with her very basic

Spanish, knew what had been said: *Sebastián, please don't say that.*

And such was the rasp in Carmen's voice that José looked over. They switched rapidly back to English—or rather Sebastián did, his voice low, clipped and authoritative.

'Get up and ask your father to dance. And even if you have to glue your teeth together, smile and talk to Maria.'

No one, Anna noted, referred to her as *Mother*.

'Never!' Carmen said, with Spanish passion. 'I would rather die.'

'Very well. You can regret it when Papá dies, then,' Sebastián said, his voice low and harsh. 'Grow up, Carmen. We can all play a part for one night.'

His stern lecture worked, because Carmen flicked back her long black hair and somehow forced a smile as she got up and went over to her father, holding out her hand. 'Papá?'

Jose was clearly tired, but his face lit up at the invitation. He was more than delighted to get up and dance with his daughter.

'I apologise for speaking over you,' Sebastián said, and Anna turned her head in surprise.

'It's not a problem.'

'Watch this,' he said darkly, and she turned her eyes from his beautiful face and watched as—of course—Maria moved over to join in with José and Carmen.

'Good girl,' Sebastián said under his breath, when Carmen didn't flounce off but instead danced with both her parents.

How rich his praise was, Anna thought.

'You adore your father,' she said.

'Not always.' Sebastián shook his head. 'I love Carmen, though, and I don't want her to regret things if she ignores him tonight.'

'Is he very ill? Emily said he's just had surgery.'

'It went well.' He gave a tight shrug. 'But, as I just said to my sister, there won't be many more celebrations like this. I am never going to be married, nor have children.'

'That sounds very certain.'

'More certain than the sun rising tomorrow,' he confirmed. 'And given that Carmen just broke up with…' He screwed up his nose in distaste, no doubt referring to Carmen's ex. 'Perhaps a christening, though?' He gave her a smile that said again that he was certain of the reason for this wedding. 'Who knows?'

He really was the best man, working for peace and harmony behind the scenes, thought Anna. Emily constantly criticised him, and although Anna completely understood why—after all, he had done everything he could to break the happy couple up—there was a lot her friend didn't see.

The faultlessness of the wedding preparations… how he'd danced with his mother just to stop her spoiling Emily's night…how he'd insisted Carmen get up and at least appear to be celebrating. How he took the time to talk to a woman who was here without friends…

Anna knew it was simply out of duty, but she admired it all the same.

'Are you close to *your* family?' he asked.

Anna gave a vague nod, but it faded, and she found herself answering more honestly than she'd intended. 'I used to be…' She felt the threat of tears when she thought of how it once had been. 'Not now.'

She could have amended her words and said that Willow was now her family, and she considered Emily to be a sister of sorts, but she couldn't do that without crying and she refused to do that.

Or she could have qualified what she'd said and say that they would be close again if she would just apologise for her behaviour and repent, voice regret… But to do so would mean she'd have to declare that she regretted Willow, and she would not do that.

Damn! She was going to cry.

She reached for her glass of champagne, or a napkin, or for her bag—perhaps she'd make a dash to the ladies'—but her fingers met his hand instead.

'Dance?'

'I don't think—'

'Come on,' he said. 'We have to keep this party going.'

'You take your duties very seriously.'

'I do,' he said, as he pulled her to her feet and onto the dance floor. They swayed politely, his hand holding one of hers, the other on her waist. 'Tomorrow I will get back to telling my brother what a fool he is.'

'You'd have preferred he married Mariana?'

'Of course. A sensible marriage that would have made good business sense. None of this love nonsense.'

'So why don't you marry Mariana, if it makes such good business sense?'

'I would never tie myself to one person,' he told her. 'Also, Mariana would expect children.'

A change in the music halted their conversation. There was more clapping and stamping, and a lot more shouts of *'Olé!'* that should have sent her scuttling back to her seat, and yet it no longer mattered that she couldn't dance, because his fluid movements made up for it.

There was serious music being made, and for the first time in her life Anna was being partnered by a man who could seriously move. He even dipped her, and then, when the music calmed again, to a slower tempo, he pulled her in close.

'See?' he said as he held her.

'See what?' Anna asked, wondering if in her daze she'd missed something he'd said.

'We move well together.'

'I think that's all you.'

'How are the heels?' he asked.

Why did he make her smile so much? 'Agony.'

'Lean on me, then,' he said, pulling her in even closer.

Her head was close to his chest now, and his hand was a little higher on her waist, and for Anna it felt as if he had located her dimmer switch and was slowly cranking it up and up. The energy that had been crackling away since she saw him at the airport was starting to spark and ignite now.

Then he lowered his head so that his deep voice was solely for her. *"'If the shoe fits, the foot is forgotten...'"*

Her mind felt misty, his words taking a moment to appear in the haze of being held by him and the low throb of his voice.

She did her best to sound unaffected and raised her head to meet his eyes. 'Did you just make that up yourself?'

'Yes,' he said, and then smiled to tell her he was fibbing. 'No, it was Zhuangzi.'

'I like that,' Anna said, hoping she could remember the quote and then resting her head on his chest. He smelt divine—of bergamot and citrus and, yes, smoke too.

Then she felt the slight stroke of his hand on her ribs.

'Do you like that?' he said, and she knew he was referring to the hand that was doing a lot more than politely resting on her waist as part of a duty dance.

She hadn't been intimate with anyone since Willow's father, and his hands had never caressed her so slowly, so lightly, so seductively. How could that slight brush of his fingers make her want to sink in, to lean in, to stretch her neck upwards and find his mouth?

'Yes,' she said—because she did like it.

This dance seemed to be an education in itself, for he was teaching her something she had not known before: that a palm on the small of her back could cause a tension so low in her stomach that it made her weak in the knees...that the fabric of a jacket could feel too warm against her cheek—so much so that she ached for the crisp white cotton of his shirt, and yet when he shifted so that her cheek rested there it still it did not suffice.

Now she wished her burning cheek was on his skin...

Anna found herself pondering the body beneath the suit, and that was most unlike her. Would he have chest hair? She couldn't imagine Sebastián being waxed, or bothering with laser treatments. He felt like more of a man than she had ever thought she might want.

'Look at me, Anna,' he said.

She had to peel herself back from his chest to do so, but, oh, he was stunning. His jaw was dusty with new growth now, and his facial symmetry was perfection.

Sebastián Romero was, quite simply, the most

beautiful man she had ever seen in the flesh. And she wanted to kiss him. Desperately.

'We would move very well together.'

She frowned, unsure if she'd misread his meaning. But, no, she looked into black eyes that beckoned her into bed.

'Excuse me?' Anna said, affronted—or rather trying to be, because in his arms she didn't quite know who she was. 'I leave tomorrow.'

'That gives us tonight.'

If it had been anyone else she'd have turned on her heel and walked off, or slapped his cheek, or...

But it wasn't anyone else.

He made the inconceivable—a one-night stand—somehow seem viable.

Anna felt the pull to step into a new persona.

And she felt danger. Not the type where your hair stands on end in fear, or your heart pounds at the prospect of imminent disaster. It was more that she felt the danger of recklessness calling to her. Because instead of walking away, she remained in his arms.

Anna felt flustered. Indignant. Curious. Bewildered...

'We haven't even kissed,' she pointed out.

'I can remedy that now, if you like.'

'No!'

Yet still she didn't walk off. Instead, her burning face returned to his chest.

One night...

It should offend her—it *had* offended her—but now the initial sting of indignation had gone his response played over and over in her head as they continued to dance.

A remedy.

This night felt exactly like that. A remedy. Dancing, laughing, flirting, wanting…

Anna hadn't dated in years. There were slim pickings in the village. Aside from her being a single mother, there was so much gossip—as well as the fact that her father was the local vicar…

There was the internet… And yet she couldn't imagine paying a babysitter and leaving Willow to go and meet someone she'd met online.

'Everything you do reflects on us.'

That had been the mantra repeated to her since before she could walk—and, given she'd let her parents down so badly, and had been so badly let down herself, Anna was now cautious to the extreme.

But she was in Spain for one more night, and Willow was safe at home…

There was a refreshing simplicity in that it could only be one night…that it could only be *this* night…

Anna was curious too, because she didn't recognise her own body and its response to his touch…

'Don't look now,' Sebastián said, breaking into her decadent thoughts, 'but the bride is looking worried.'

Anna jolted to attention. 'If something's wrong, I should go.'

'Shh…' He pulled her closer into him. '*We* are what is wrong,'

'Oh.'

'Emily is not a fan of mine.'

'I'd worked that out.'

'Why don't we finish this dance now?' he said in a low, deep voice. 'Then I will dance with a few others and you will do the same.'

'Okay…'

'But don't dance with them like this,' he warned.

'I don't think I could dance like this with anyone else,' came her honest response, for it felt to her as though their bodies were melded together.

'*Maldita!*' he said, as if her words had hollowed him. 'I don't want to let you go…'

It was necessary, though, and not just to put Emily off the scent. Seriously, if they did not part now then they would have to kiss, so painfully did her mouth ache for his.

'You know where my suite is,' he said as the music faded.

'I don't,' she denied.

'Anna, you saw me go in.'

She screwed her eyes closed, but the vision of that wooden door he had walked through last night was burnt into her mind.

Anna felt cold on this hot Spanish night when he let her go.

Bewildered.

Excited.

Things she had never felt before.

She walked back to the table and took a long drink of iced water, and sure enough Emily was over in a couple of moments, looking concerned.

'What's going on with you and Sebastián?'

'I was just dancing with the best man.'

'Come off it.' Emily's eyes were wide. 'Anna, do *not* fall for his slick charm. He's an utter bastard. He spits out women like olive pips.'

Though she winced inwardly, Anna kept her response light. 'He's a brilliant dancer, Emily, that's all.' She looked in Sebastián's direction and, sure enough, he was dancing with a gorgeous raven-haired woman. 'He's working the room.'

'I'd just hate you to get hurt.'

'Emily, it's your wedding. Please don't worry about me. It's going great, isn't it?'

'It is, but we're about to head off. Although I think the party will go on for ages. Don't forget— breakfast in the hotel with the family tomorrow.'

And then back to the real world.

Emily continued, 'Oh, Anna, I'm so pleased you're here.'

'As if I'd miss your wedding!'

Anna felt a stab of guilt, because had her mother refused to look after Willow then she would have missed it. Of course she would never tell Emily that. Perhaps when she had her own baby she might understand the constant push and pull of motherhood—it would have been hell to miss Emily's wedding, but Willow came first.

Willow would *always* come first.

And, because of that, she hadn't danced or been held in four years. Then she amended that thought. She hadn't *ever* danced or been held the way Sebastián had danced with her and held her...

There was cheering and clapping as the happy couple headed out through the gorgeous cellar, waving to their guests and moving into the plaza, where they were sent off with more cheering and good wishes, and then the exuberant Spaniards turned back to party on in the bodega.

Returning to the party, even though it remained lively and noisy, Anna knew immediately that Sebastián had gone...

'Would you like to dance?' a young man invited, but Anna politely declined.

She didn't want to dance with anyone else. She knew absolutely that it would never be as good as the dance she'd shared with Sebastián.

She walked out of the bodega in heels that now really hurt and tried not to notice again the stained-glass windows that reminded her of a church...

As if serving her a warning...

Anna sighed as she acknowledged it.

She would not be spending the night with Sebastián.

She stepped out into the square and walked past the stunning water fountain towards the hotel. The concierge gave her a nod, and the night porter greeted her and pulled back the heavy metal doors of the elevator that would take her up to her suite.

Tonight they reminded her of the bars of a prison.

And Sebastián had offered her one night of pure freedom...

'Perdóneme,' she said, blushing as she turned away from the lift and walked across the reception area before turning to the left towards the arched wooden door.

It was unlocked, so she opened it, then stepped into what looked like a forbidden garden. It was another courtyard, with romantic Spanish music playing and soft lights twinkling.

And waiting to greet her as she entered was Sebastián.

He had removed his shirt and tie and she discovered she had been right: he didn't wax or shave.

Goodness, he was stunning...

'Now,' he said, walking over to her and then dropping to his knees and removing her shoes, 'we can dance as we want.'

CHAPTER FOUR

THE RELIEF OF shedding her shoes was nothing compared to the relief of his naked skin on her cheek.

No, not relief…

She was shaking as his hand went to her underarm zipper and slid it down.

'Did your friend warn you about me?'

'She did.'

Her voice was unfamiliar, shaky with lust, and when his mouth found hers she almost sobbed in relief.

He parted her lips further with his tongue, deep kissing her hard, and Anna found a side to herself she had never known before. Because her hands shot to his head and then she was gripping and twisting his silky black hair as she came alive beneath the demands of his mouth.

Sebastián did not have to coax reluctant lips. He lit a flame inside Anna that had previously been unknown to her. For once she was, oh, so very willing.

'I've wanted to kiss you all night,' he said. 'Since yesterday, in fact.'

He picked her up and carried her through the courtyard. She kissed him all the way to the bed, stopping only as he put her down on the cover.

She lay breathless, her mouth swollen from their

kisses and her body taut with arousal as he looked down on her.

'I'm going to undress you now,' he said, pushing the skirt of her dress to her waist and skimming his hands along her thighs.

She sat up and raised her arms as he removed the dress, and there was not a whisper of anything other than bliss as he draped it carelessly over a nearby chair.

He unhooked her strapless bra and reverently touched one breast while he kissed her hot cheek. But just as Anna closed her eyes and lay back down, to enjoy the bliss of his touch, he removed his hand.

He focused his attention on sliding her knickers off, and Anna was surprised to find that she did not feel her usual shyness at being naked. Instead, she revelled in his dark stare and the way his breathing quickened as he looked down at her.

'Anna?'

'Yes?'

'You made the day better.'

'You did too.'

'Not just because of this,' he said as he unbuckled his belt.

'I know,' she replied.

For she knew what he meant. His presence, however temporary, had made her feel better too. She had really enjoyed their time together. All of it.

She propped herself up on her elbows so she

could admire his naked body—his strong arms and his long, muscular, hairy legs. She tightened her jaw as she looked at the magnificent erection that rose from him, and any lingering shyness was forgotten as she sat up and reached over to where he stood.

His hair was like fine silk, Anna thought as she touched first the black strands on his stomach and then moved her hand down and held him, stroked him, explored him for a moment, before he stepped away from her hand.

He took a condom from the bedside table and she watched as he carefully rolled it down. She lay back, fizzing with anticipation.

'I'm going to kiss you everywhere later...' he said as he knelt on all fours on the vast bed.

'So will I you,' she whispered, in a seductive tone she'd never heard from herself before.

And then she just sank into the bliss of their naked kiss.

The need he had exposed in her continued to rise as his thighs parted hers. She was ready...so ready!

The bliss of him entering her was sublime, and as he pushed up onto his forearms he stared down and started to move deep within her.

'You feel fantastic.'

Anna could hear the little panting sobs she was making. 'I'm crying!' she said with a breathless laugh.

'Because now you can give in.'

'Yes.'

She was giving in to her body and so was he to his, because he began to thrust faster and faster, and her small sobs turned to moans of treacle-thick desire.

'Yes!' she said again, but to what she didn't know.

His breathing was ragged, in time with their movements, and then he thrust one final time—hard and fast—and stilled. His shout was the most welcome sound. It was as if her body recognised it…as if her energy raced to meet his, hurtled towards an intimate centre where she was locked with him, pulsing around him, so that they were released together.

'*Dios…*' he said, as if he were dizzy.

For a moment perhaps he was dizzy, because he did not want to pull out. He wanted to rock them slowly back to a second pleasure. But he was too careful for that and instead slowly withdrew.

'You okay?' he asked as they lay in the soft glow of twinkling lights and he pulled her against him.

'Very.' Anna nodded. 'Though I don't want anyone—'

'Anna,' he interrupted. 'I don't discuss my life with anyone.'

Not with *anyone*.

And yet he was aware that he had spoken rather too freely with her already.

This had been an impossible day, made better by Anna. It was rare that he dropped his guard, and he never dropped it as much as he had with the intoxicating woman in his arms. He had told her more about his family than he usually would. More about himself.

Sebastián knew he needed to halt this now.

'Anna...'

He stopped, because he didn't know what he was going to say. She didn't answer anyway, and he realised she was asleep.

He started to remove his arm, because he did not do the 'lying together afterwards' thing—he could not, would not, allow himself to do that. And yet he left his arm there, and thought he would close his eyes just for a moment...

It was a couple of hours later when he finally removed his arm, then climbed out of bed and headed to the shower, knowing he had got too close, knowing she had affected him too much...

But why?

Anna woke—but only because the real world was waking too.

She heard the buzz of her phone and saw there were several missed calls from Willow.

'Darling,' she said. 'How are you this morning?'

'We're going to church,' Willow said. 'For *two* services.'

'Ooh!' Anna smiled, remembering it well. 'Well,

I'm going for breakfast and then heading to the airport. I'll be in the air and on my way back to you by the time you're leaving church.'

'Really?'

'Yes.'

They chatted about the wedding for a bit longer, and then she heard her mother calling for Willow.

'I'll be home before you know it,' Anna said, and then listened to another minute of excited chatter before Willow said she had to go. 'I love you, my darling,' Anna said.

Unfortunately it was just as Sebastián came out of the shower, and she saw a look flash across his face.

'Sebastián…' She ran a hand through her hair. 'That's not… That wasn't—'

'It's fine.' He shrugged. 'You don't have to explain. We both know it's one night…'

'No!' She didn't want to leave things like that. 'That was my daughter—Willow.'

Sebastián met her eyes then, and for reasons he couldn't fathom right now realised he'd possibly have preferred to be her illicit lover. He understood that she might have hidden the fact she had a partner, but as he looked at the rumpled bed and her body he realised that, for all they had shared over the past day or so, she hadn't once hinted that she was a mother.

He felt lied to.

'You never said.'

He thought of how he had taken care of his baby sister and younger brother when Maria went on her endless tours, and how conveniently she'd forgotten she had three children at home…

There was a cheap shot, forming in the dark corners of his mind: 'Out of sight, out of mind, is it?'

Yes, a very cheap shot, but he said it anyway.

Anna felt as if she had been turned to stone. It wasn't just the words—it was the malice with which they'd been said.

'I wasn't aware we were trading life stories.'

She awkwardly pulled on her dress and picked up her shoes, not even attempting to strap them on for her walk of shame back to her hotel room.

She seethed in silence, but turned back to him as she opened the door. 'If I were a man it wouldn't be an issue.'

He stared back at her but said nothing.

'Chauvinist p—!'

Anna halted abruptly. She'd been about to say *pig*, but she never used language like that and wasn't about to do it now.

'Thanks for a great night,' she said dryly, and walked out.

Breakfast was hell.

The Romeros and the De Lucas and all their guests attacked the food with relish. Anna merely drank strong coffee and nibbled a pastry and felt shaken inside.

Sebastián's sense of duty was clearly over, because he declared himself too hungover to drive Anna to the airport and quickly arranged for a driver to take her instead.

'Thank you, my dearest friend.' Emily hugged her goodbye. 'I wish you could stay longer.'

'I'm sure you don't.' Anna smiled. 'You've got a honeymoon to get to…and we'll get together soon.'

She kissed Alejandro on the cheek and waved to the other guests.

Sebastián didn't so much as look up.

She bristled at the feeling of having had her commitment to motherhood challenged by Sebastián—and then felt guilty as hell on the plane ride home.

Despite what her parents thought about Willow's conception, she had never had a one-night stand in her life. Willow's father had been a visiting professor during Anna's final year at university and, unused to male attention, Anna had thought for a time it might be love.

Unable to believe how immature she had been back then, Anna snorted, and the man sitting next to her jumped.

She turned and looked out of the plane window at the grey clouds forming and amended that thought: how inexperienced she had been *until last night*. Oh, all her feelings for her ex had long since been severed, but until last night he'd been her one and only lover.

When she arrived back home, and was sitting in the kitchen of the vicarage where she'd grown up, she put on a bland face and ate a rather stale scone. But inside she felt reckless and wild, unable to believe that last night she'd slept with a man she barely knew… And she felt gullible too, because she'd honestly thought they'd connected on a deeper level…that her friend was wrong in her opinion of him.

Yet it would seem that Emily had been right. His sudden contempt had made her feel abandoned and rejected, like she had with her ex. Discarded.

And the most confusing part…

The hardest part…

Her one night with Sebastián had been the most exciting night of her life.

And now she knew exactly what she'd been missing all these years.

CHAPTER FIVE

Unforgettable...

Despite their awful parting, her encounter with Sebastián was something she couldn't shake off or forget—and not just because Emily soon sent a link to the wedding photos.

Her daughter snuggled on her knee while they went through the images.

'Who's that?' Willow asked, pointing straight at the glamorous Maria, dressed in her flamenco regalia.

'That's Maria,' Anna explained. 'She's Emily's mother-in-law and a famous flamenco dancer.'

'I want to be a flamenco dancer *so* badly,' Willow sighed.

'I know!' Anna laughed, because Willow had put on the garish green flamenco dress that Emily had bought her just to look at the pictures.

'Is that Alejandro?' Willow pointed to a tall, dark and exceptionally good-looking man.

'No, that's his brother,' Anna responded casually.

She hastily clicked on to the next image, but there was no escape there—it was a picture of her and Sebastián standing next to each other in the vestry.

She had been so acutely aware of him in that moment, Anna thought. Her arm had still been recovering from the lightest touch of his fingers, and if she allowed herself to she could close her eyes and capture again the sharp, clean scent of the cologne that enhanced the essence of the man.

'What's his name?' Willow asked. 'The brother?'

'Sebastián,' Anna said, curiously relieved to say his name out loud.

His impact had been so strong, it felt almost as if it had left some kind of residue behind.

From that day forward, every night, when Willow had gone to bed, Anna resisted the urge to look at those photos. She would pick up her sewing, or the blanket she was embroidering for Emily and Alejandro's baby, but it was like knowing there were chocolate biscuits in the tin...

Sometimes she would put her sewing down and sit in her little garden on warm summer evenings, breathing in the scent of lavender, trying to escape the memories of him and hating him for that final one.

And it wasn't just the evenings when there were too many moments when he came to mind—no, he popped into her head at the most random times.

Once, busy at work, she'd slipped off a shoe under her desk, just to wiggle her toes, and that simple, unthinking motion had taken her mind straight back to him.

She'd looked up the quote from Zhuangzi.

When the shoe fits, the foot is forgotten; when the belt fits, the belly is forgotten. When the heart is right, 'for' and 'against' are forgotten.

No drives, no compulsions, no needs, no attractions: Then your affairs are under control. You are a free man.

Anna felt she didn't quite get it, and yet she set it as the wallpaper on her phone.

Sex, she now knew, had been dreadful with Willow's father. But it wasn't just the soul-shaking sex with Sebastián that she yearned for, it was the smiles and the honesty—well, apart from her omission about Willow—and how it hadn't felt like bitching when they'd shared their mutual concern about the haste of the wedding.

Needless concern, it would seem, because Emily and Alejandro were besotted and eagerly awaiting the arrival of their baby—though Emily kept inviting Anna to come out and see her.

And now Willow was having her surgery, and although it was just a day case, Anna felt grateful that her mother had come too, and was there in the waiting room when she had to let go of Willow's hand as she was wheeled off after having been put under anaesthetic.

Things were getting better with her mother.

It still wasn't brilliant between them, but she knew her parents adored Willow, and now, as she sat with her mother in the hospital waiting room, Jean Douglas surprised her.

She was talking about her and father's annual trip to Scotland, to visit cousins and aunts there. Anna was only half listening, her eyes on the door, waiting to hear that Willow's surgery was done and her daughter was well.

'…if Willow might like to come? A little holiday before she starts school?'

Anna turned and looked at her mother, who repeated what she'd been saying. The invitation was clearly for Willow only. Jean didn't want her single mother daughter too much on show with the cousins, but apparently her granddaughter was acceptable.

Then her mother surprised her again. 'You could maybe go and see Emily.'

'Really?' Anna checked.

'I know you miss her, and…' Jean gave a tight shrug. 'Well, it's something to think about.'

Then a doctor in scrubs came to the door and smiled, and for a while summer and holidays were forgotten.

Her mother raised it again a couple of weeks later, and Anna realised it had been more than an idle suggestion. They *really* wanted to take Willow with them, and Willow *really* wanted to go.

Emily was thrilled when Anna called.

'Oh, my goodness. Yes!'

'Seven nights,' Anna said. 'I'd arrive on Saturday and leave on the following Sunday, if that's okay?'

'I can't wait!'

At six months pregnant, Emily clearly wanted to show off her lovely tummy and see her friend.

'Alejandro keeps asking when you'll be out to visit. He's having to travel a lot, but that's so he can take time off when the baby arrives.'

'How have things been?' Anna asked. 'With the family?'

'José seems to be doing well, although Maria's still rubbing everyone up the wrong way. She's moved back into the family home, so Carmen's incensed.'

And...? Anna wanted to ask. *What about Sebastián?*

But she didn't want to give even the slightest hint she might be remotely interested. As well as that, she wasn't entirely convinced that Emily didn't already know. So she listened as Emily asked about Willow.

'Next time bring her. Honestly, once I have the baby it will be so much fun for us all to be together.'

But then finally, near the end of their conversation, Anna got a little sliver of the information she was desperate to hear.

'Bloody Sebastián,' Emily said. 'Honestly, he's off on his yacht...barely here...'

'Things are no better between you guys?'

'To be honest, I hardly see him.'

Anna saw him every time she closed her eyes...

Life for Anna was expensive, with school starting soon for Willow, as well as new clothes for her holiday in Scotland. Add to that a flight to Spain, and things were tight.

Emily had offered to pay for the flight, but Anna didn't want things to be like that between them. She would be staying with her and Alejandro, so wouldn't have to worry about accommodation.

She had saved hard, and had an emergency fund, but would prefer not to dip into that—after all, a holiday was hardly an emergency. And by trimming all excess off her own holiday wardrobe—apart from a gorgeous red bikini and a red and white sarong that had been on sale at the supermarket—plus the help of her sewing machine, Anna had managed to keep the emergency fund intact.

Come mid-August, she sat with Willow as they both packed their cases. Anna carefully added the blanket she had so painstakingly embroidered for the baby. Usually sewing was her means to relax, but since Sebastián had arrived and then so swiftly departed from her life she'd had to fight hard just to concentrate on the basics.

'Are you going to give Emily the blanket now?' Willow asked, and Anna nodded. 'But she hasn't had the baby.'

'I'd like to give it to her myself,' Anna said, 'and I won't see her again for a while.'

She looked at her gorgeous daughter, who didn't have a jealous bone in her body and was simply happy that her mum was going on holiday too.

'We'll go to Spain together next time,' Anna promised.

Willow gave a squeal of delight. 'Can Nanny and Grandpa come?'

'Just us.' Anna smiled. 'We'll have our own little holiday and see the baby.'

A delighted Willow skipped off to find some hair ties to put in her little toiletry bag and Anna added the bikini and sarong to her case. It had looked so pretty in the shop, but in natural light the colour was more violet than red…an ugly kind of pink…

Anna laughed to herself, remembering Sebastián's opinion of Mariana's dress at the wedding. He was still a constant in her thoughts. She was nervous about the possibility of seeing Sebastián when she was in Spain, but tried to console herself that he would probably be out on his yacht and their paths would not cross at all.

It didn't feel like a consolation, though.

'What are these?' Willow asked, standing at the bedroom door holding a slim, shiny foil package of pills.

'Willow,' Anna said calmly, 'you know better than to touch someone else's medicine.'

'Medicine?' Willow frowned. 'Are you ill?'

Possibly in the head, Anna thought. Because there was no way she could justify, even to herself, her recent trip to the doctor to get the contraceptive Pill.

You hate him, she'd reminded herself.

And she hated herself every morning when she took a tiny tablet.

And yet she wanted him still.

He fascinated and confused her, and he angered her too, but most of all she couldn't get that flash out of her mind—the look that had darted across his face when he'd heard her say 'I love you, my darling' to what he'd thought was another man.

On the morning both Willow and Anna were to depart, she dropped her daughter off at the vicarage.

Anna wore the same long skirt and flat sandals she had the last time she'd flown to Spain, but with a high-necked sleeveless top and the silver earrings that Emily had bought for her birthday.

'That's a bit dressed up for flying,' her mother commented, when she saw the sleeveless top and jewellery.

Anna didn't respond, just told her that Willow already had her travel sickness band on, ready for the car.

'Mummy's got travel sickness tablets too,' Willow declared.

'You've never been travel sick,' her father said, frowning.

'Just when I fly.' Anna hid her blush by dropping to her knees to hug her daughter goodbye. 'Have fun,' she said as she held her. 'And be good for Nanny and Grandpa.'

'Do I have to be good *all* the time?' Willow pouted.

Even Jean laughed.

Willow was a light in all their lives, and Anna kissed and hugged her fiercely.

Her father, who had always been gentler than her mother, announced her imminent departure. 'Your taxi's here,' he said as he hoisted Willow onto his hip and gave Anna a kiss. 'Don't let me mix up your suitcases!' he teased as he picked up one to take it out to the car. 'Give our love to Emily and her husband.'

'I will.'

Her mother's farewell was less effusive, even though she gave her a small kiss on the cheek, she offered a parting shot as she walked down the path. 'Make good choices, Anna.'

Anna felt her back stiffen. She wanted to turn around and say something—to point out that she was twenty-six and not a teenager going off to a school disco. Instead, she took a deep breath and decided, as she always did for the sake of peace, to just let it go.

She'd made only one terrible choice that they knew of, Anna thought as she waved goodbye to them all, but especially to Willow, whom she knew would wave until she was out of sight.

And just look at the gorgeous consequence.

The other terrible choice…

Anna took out her phone and looked at the quote.

She thought of Sebastián and the wedding.

And still she did not regret it. For in their short time together he had taught her so much about how good sex with the right man could be.

Apart from the cruel parting.

Just to be safe, and so as not to appear pathetic if he inadvertently saw it, she deleted the quote from her phone.

On the flight she tried to focus on a biography she'd been saving to read but, gritty though it was, she couldn't focus. Instead she felt butterflies leaping in her stomach and chest, accompanying her all the way to Seville.

Anna walked out of Arrivals at Seville, trying to forget the last time she had done so, and trying not to recollect how she and Sebastián had locked eyes, and the little joke he'd played, telling her that she'd got the wrong man.

Looking around for her friend, she was suddenly startled. She must be imagining things...because it couldn't be him.

Him.

Sebastián.

This time he was unshaven, and his hair was longer than she remembered, and he was wearing black trousers and a pale grey rumpled linen shirt.

Maybe by some coincidence he was here to meet someone else—but, no, he put one hand up when he saw her.

Anna's first thought was that he was too suave to wave.

Her second—selfish—thought was that she wished she wasn't wearing the same skirt and sandals he'd seen her in before.

But then the nerves set in.

If he was here then something must be wrong!

Telling herself that there were a hundred reasons why Alejandro might have asked Sebastián to pick up his wife's friend, she made her way over to the man who had haunted her dreams for weeks.

'Hey,' he said as she approached.

He must have seen her frown, then appear confused, and then seen her eyes widen in sudden concern that something might be wrong with her friend, because he was quick to reassure her.

'It's okay. Everything is okay.'

He touched her bare arm, but clearly things were not okay—because if they were, given how they had parted, *he* would not be here.

'Where's Emily?' Anna asked, desperately hoping to be further reassured.

But when he paused before answering she knew that there was something amiss.

'In hospital. The baby is not behaving.'

Anna swallowed.

'She was taken into hospital earlier. You were in the air by then, and Alejandro asked if I would collect you.'

The fact that his hand was still on her arm told Anna that there was more.

'Alejandro has just called and said she's about to be flown to Marbella, as there is an intensive care neonatal unit there.'

'So they think she might have the baby? But it's too soon!' Anna's heart leapt into her throat.

'I don't know any more than that.'

He must have become aware that he was still touching her arm, because he dropped contact and stepped back just a fraction.

Anna stood, her head spinning with the news.

What should she do?

Should she fly to Marbella, or would she only be in the way?

Should she change her flight and just turn around and go home?

'She was there when I had Wi—'

Anna stopped, feeling the stinging hurt he had caused the last time she had mentioned her daughter return. She absolutely would not be discussing her daughter with this man.

'Thank you,' she said. 'For coming to the airport and telling me.'

'What do you want to do?' he asked.

'I'll work it out.'

'I don't think I'm supposed to report back and say I left you here *working it out*.'

Anna looked up, and although he looked back

at her he did not quite meet her eyes. She guessed this must be the very last place he wanted to be.

'I'm driving up to Marbella,' he informed her. 'You're welcome to join me. I'm getting my yacht moved and docked there, but in the meantime I'll get my PA to sort out accommodation.'

Anna instantly shook her head, well aware that she couldn't afford any hotel that a Romero would stay at. But surely she'd be able to find somewhere cheaper once she got there, as well as change her return flight. She couldn't really deal with the logistics right now. All she could think of was that her best friend's baby was possibly about to be born too soon.

'I don't know what to do,' she admitted.

He made the decision for her.

'Come on,' he said. 'You'll drive up with me. You can change your return flight when we know more.'

His was the voice of reason, so she nodded and started to walk.

'Your case,' he reminded her, but didn't retrieve it himself. The kid gloves were clearly off.

The silver car was familiar this time. 'How far is it to Marbella?' she asked.

'A couple of hours,' he said, and then amended the time frame. 'Maybe two and a half if I have a tense passenger.'

Of course he had a tense passenger, after the

way they had parted and now Emily's situation was so precarious.

They drove in silence for a considerable while, during which Anna's mind was going in every direction.

'Anna, could we discuss—?'

'No.' She cut him off, because she could not discuss that horrible morning—especially as she was sure now that were it not for this emergency she wouldn't even have seen him once on this trip.

Her phone buzzed and Anna quickly swiped to answer it. She saw it was Emily.

'Em!'

Sebastián listened to the one-sided conversation and heard her calm, upbeat voice, though he could see that her knee was bobbing up and down.

'That's good. Give the medication some time to work...'

There was a pause while she listened.

'Don't worry, I'm in the car with Sebastián...'

And another.

'It doesn't matter if I'm not allowed in to see you. Just stay calm...'

And finally, 'Love you too.'

Then the call ended and she passed on the little news she had.

'They're trying to stop the labour and they've given her some medicine for the baby's lungs, just in case, but things seem better now than this morning.'

'Okay,' he said, and then he glanced over. 'Anna, I just want to say that I was wrong—'

'I do *not* want to talk about that morning,' she said firmly.

'What…?' He looked over again. 'You think *that's* what I want to discuss?'

'Just watch the road.'

'I was about to say that I was wrong in what I said about Emily and Alejandro. They are happy together. Even a cynic like me can see it.'

Sebastián saw her tight shrug and also her blush.

He knew he had just bluffed his way out of a necessary conversation. The truth was he *had* been about to discuss that morning, and to apologise. But then he'd heard the raw hurt in her voice and decided that the conversation might be better conducted when he was not driving.

As well as that, after all this time he still didn't know what to say. He didn't quite understand himself why he'd reacted as sharply as he had that morning.

He breathed out in frustration—but then his assistant called and told him where she had made reservations and gave him the exclusive address.

'I've booked you a beachfront room,' she told him. 'What do you want for your companion?' she asked.

'I'll sort it when we arrive,' Sebastián said, then clicked off.

As they zipped through mountainous countryside Anna was embarrassed to have assumed that their bitter parting was at the forefront of his mind, and was relieved when her phone buzzed again, to break the tense silence. But then she saw that it was Willow.

'Hello, darling!' Anna attempted to sound upbeat. 'I'm in a car,' she said, smiling deliberately and hoping it might show in her voice. 'How's Scotland?'

'Is Emily there?' Willow asked. 'Can I talk to her?'

'Not now because we're still driving, Willow,' Anna said. 'What are you up to?'

She spoke for several minutes, and reassured her daughter that she'd send some photos when she could, and then finally said goodbye.

'We're almost there,' Sebastián informed her as they came around a bend.

And there was the sparkling blue of the Mediterranean stretched out before them.

Anna didn't say anything at first, just looked at the sun-drenched view, knowing that somewhere down there was Emily, and that her friend was feeling scared.

Then the car turned and they drove parallel to the bright sea. She looked out at the yachts and expensive cars and the sheer glamour of the place.

When he'd said Marbella, she hadn't really known what to think.

But then she saw a sign for Puerto Banús and felt her chest tighten. Anna knew this place was way over her budget. She looked at the huge, luxurious residences, the ridiculously flashy cars and snow-white yachts, silently willing him to drive further on, past the golden mile.

It was not to be, though, for his car slowed and the indicator clicked.

He pulled into the beautiful gated grounds of a hotel shaded with palm trees and not a high-rise in sight.

Anna shook her head. 'I'm going to need to find somewhere a little more…' *Or rather, a lot less.*

But Sebastián was having none of it, and he told her so before she got out of the car.

'Don't be ridiculous. Nobody's expecting you to pay. We are—'

'I am *not* sharing a room with you.'

'Believe me, I wasn't offering,' he said.

Well, that told her!

'We are close to the hospital here,' Sebastián said, 'and for now that's the only concern.'

'I don't want you paying for me.'

'I'll charge it to my brother, then. Don't make an issue when there isn't one,' he said. 'But feel free to wander off in the heat and find a hostel, just to make your point.'

She moved to get out of the car, but suddenly it all caught up with her. Emily must be so scared, and the baby was at risk, and Willow would be in Scotland for a whole week… And then there was the shock of being met by *him*.

Anna did the last thing she wanted to do and leant back in the car seat and started to cry…

She saw him wave away the approaching bellboy and he remained seated beside her and did nothing, for which Anna was actually grateful. Because she knew that if he touched her arm again—or, heaven forbid, *held her*—she'd howl.

'I have no handkerchief to offer,' he finally said, as she rummaged in her bag.

Somehow he managed to force a smile, and Anna knew she had to swallow both her tears and her pride. She found a tissue to mop her tears and nodded. 'I'll stay tonight…until we know more about Emily.'

'Good.' Sebastián nodded.

He too was struggling. Tears usually didn't move him in the least, yet he sensed hers were rare, and it killed him just to sit there and do nothing. He'd heard the anger in her tone, though, and doubted any attempt to comfort her would be welcome.

As well as that, he did not do *comfort*.

'Why don't we get checked in?' Sebastián suggested. 'And then we can get the hell away from each other…'

'Yes, okay. Good idea.'

They entered a very cool air-conditioned lobby. So cool that the receptionist wore a smart blazer and full make-up and looked as if she'd stepped off the cover of a glossy magazine.

'Señor Romano.' She smiled and welcomed him. *'Bienvenido de vuelta!'*

The admin was all speedily dealt with, but something the receptionist said caused him to respond with a very blunt, *'No.'*

He explained it to Anna as they walked past a sign indicating *habitaciones contiguas.* 'She asked if we wanted adjoining villas.'

'No!' Anna repeated with the same blunt edge to her voice.

They walked beneath palm trees and he told her to order whatever she wanted to the villa, then added, 'Breakfast on the terrace is nice here, though. It's down that way.'

'Okay…'

'This is you,' he said, and handed her a folder that held a card to open the door to her villa.

'Where are you?'

'Down there.' He pointed to another path. 'I'll call you if I hear anything from the hospital.'

'Likewise.' She nodded.

'I still have your number,' he said. And then, rather reluctantly, Anna thought, added, 'I was going to text you an apology for what I said that morning.'

'Yeah, right…'

'And you were right. I *was* trying to talk about

it in the car, but then I thought it better not to discuss it on a mountainous road.'

'I don't want to discuss *anything* with you—on a mountainous road or anywhere else.'

Anna flounced off, and it was such a relief to get away from his assault to her senses that it took the edge off the sheer luxury of her home for the night.

It wasn't a room, nor even a suite. It was a gorgeous villa, with pale wooden floors and white furnishings. There was her own terrace, and a huge shower and bath, but most welcoming of all was the low bed dressed in crisp linen that tempted her to climb in.

First, though, she texted Emily and let her know that she was here. But she got no response.

Hopefully her friend was asleep, Anna thought as she had a quick shower and then put on a robe. She shut the screens to block out the turbulent day and lay in silence in the blacked-out room.

But when she closed her eyes there was still Sebastián. There was also the sound of his reluctant apology and the tartness of her own brittle response.

Of course she had lied to his face. Because there was so much she wanted to discuss with him.

She lay there, fighting fury and attraction, angry at their parting and cross with herself for how much she still liked him.

'I have no handkerchief to offer.'
Why did he still make her smile?

CHAPTER SIX

ANNA SLEPT HORRIBLY and awoke to a knock on the door. She lay there, disorientated, unsure of the time and even the day.

The knock on the door sounded again, and she wished she'd put out the 'Do Not Disturb' sign—or whatever it was in Spanish. But she pulled on a robe and went to open the door. Perhaps breakfast had arrived?

But it was only evening, she realised, and Sebastián was standing there, shaved and smartly dressed. She was about to say that he was supposed to have texted, when he told her the reason for his personal call.

'It's a girl.'

'Oh, my!'

'She seems to be doing well.' Then he clarified, 'Well, that is from Alejandro, and I don't know if he's talking sense or... Can I come in?'

Given the circumstances, she opened the door for him.

He sat on the sofa and Anna took a chair. He seemed a little stunned, but still very together as he told her the little he knew. 'Emily's okay, but I think she had to take some serious drugs, so she is very tired. The baby has a machine to help her breathe.'

'She'll be terrified,' Anna said. 'It's so early. How much does she weigh?'

'I don't know.'

'Did you even ask?' Anna snapped.

'No,' he responded calmly. 'I was more focused on reassuring my brother than asking questions.'

Suitably chastised, Anna briefly closed her eyes. It was her turn to apologise.

'Sorry.'

'No problem,' he accepted with a shrug.

'Have you told your family?'

He nodded. 'Drama, drama—as always. They want to fly up. I told them to wait. Maria will just…' He paused. 'I think Alejandro and Emily may need some time…just them.'

'Yes.'

'Alejandro asked if you are okay, and I said not to worry—that I would take you for dinner.'

'I don't want to go out.'

Certainly not with him, looking like that. He was polished…almost gleaming. He wore dark trousers and suede shoes. Gone was the crumpled shirt, replaced by white linen that illuminated his dark beauty.

'I'm not even hungry.'

'Of course—you must have eaten on the plane.'

A granola bar.

'But that was hours ago,' he added, just to make his point. 'Well, I told him we would toast the baby and send a photo to cheer up Emily.'

'That's blackmail.'

'Possibly. But I'm hungry, and I actually do think the baby should be celebrated. My father is begging them to fetch a priest, so some happy messages might be nice?'

'I get it.' Anna nodded.

She headed back into her bedroom and went through her case. She selected the dress that she'd hoped to wear on a night out with Emily. It was a dark red cotton, and loose-fitting, but it would have to do. Running a comb through her hair, she saw she looked pale in the mirror, so she put on a slick of lipstick and some blusher on her cheeks.

'That's better,' he said as she came out.

'You look nice,' she suggested, rather sarcastically.

'Thank you,' he smiled.

Anna rolled her eyes. 'I've got to call my daughter and say goodnight.'

'Of course. Do you want me to wait outside?'

Anna shot him a cool look. 'It's my daughter, Sebastián, not my lover.'

It was just a quick call, and a nice goodnight, and then her mother came to the phone and updated her on how Willow had enjoyed the journey up to Scotland. And then she asked how she was.

Anna closed her eyes and chose to lie. 'I'm good. It sounds as if you're all having a brilliant time.'

She felt Sebastián's acute interest as he noticed that she'd chosen not to tell her mother anything of the day's events, but he didn't say anything when she put her phone in her bag and said she was ready to go.

'Card to get back in?' he reminded her.

'Oh, yes.'

Under normal circumstances this place would be paradise, Anna thought. Instead of eating in the hotel restaurant they walked towards the port, where there was music and beautiful people. Sebastián fitted right in, Anna thought, as she saw many heads turn when people noticed him.

'Sebastián,' the greeter said, smiling as they walked into a beautiful restaurant and were led up to the first floor, to a gorgeous table that overlooked the stunning yachts.

Chatting easily with the sommelier, who also knew him by name, Sebastián ordered champagne.

'You're well known here,' she said.

'I come here quite often.'

He might be familiar with the surroundings, but Anna had never felt more out of place in her life. She went through the menu as the champagne was poured and wished it had prices, or a few English translations...

'Pink for a girl,' Sebastián said, and as she looked up he nodded to the sky.

It was true—the sky was every shade of pink and lilac.

Why did he have to go and be so nice?

He put their two glasses on the white balcony

ledge and took a picture of the blazing sky, then sent it to his brother.

Sebastián raised his glass. 'To her health!'

'To her health,' Anna replied, and they clinked glasses. 'Oh, and congratulations, Uncle Sebastián.'

'Thank you. Congratulations to you too...' He rarely paused in his English, but she heard him do it for a second. 'Aunty Anna.'

'Thank you.'

She took a breath and decided that she could at least make polite conversation with him, for the sake of Emily's new baby girl. She would have to whenever they saw each other in the future, and she decided she might as well start practising now.

'I'm glad I'm nearby. At first I didn't know if I should turn around and go home.'

'You and Emily are close?'

'Very.' Anna nodded. 'Since we were little. Our parents were friends.'

'Were?'

'Emily lost her parents.'

'That's right.'

'They died around the same time I fell out with mine, so...'

'You fell out with your parents?'

She nodded, but didn't elaborate, rather wishing he hadn't picked up on that.

'Why?'

'That's rather personal.'

'Fine.' He shrugged easily letting it go. 'Are you ready to order?'

She stared again at the menu, but still had no idea what she wanted.

'The mussels are incredible here,' he prompted kindly.

'Sounds lovely.'

They certainly looked incredible. It was a huge bowl of mussels, in a creamy white wine sauce waiting to be mopped up with crispy bread. And although their conversation was rather tense and awkward, Anna had a favour to ask.

'Can I ask you to take a photo of me? To send to my daughter?'

'It would be my pleasure.'

He took her phone, and she was so glad she'd deleted the picture of that quote!

'Smile,' he told her, and she tried. 'As if you mean it?' he suggested. 'Anna, please smile as if it's not me sitting opposite you.'

She laughed at that, and he captured the moment.

'There you go,' he said, and handed back the phone.

As Anna forwarded the message to Willow, Sebastián received a text of his own. 'Alejandro is checking that I am taking suitably good care of you.'

'You are,' Anna responded, and decided that now might be the right time to ask him something that had been on her mind—just get it out of the way in one go. 'Did you ever tell Alejandro?'

'Tell him what?'

'About us. About that night.'

'Anna!' He actually laughed at the very notion. 'I'm thirty-five. I don't keep my brother updated on my life, and I'm sure he has no interest in knowing who I slept with on his wedding night.'

'Okay…' She sighed out a soft laugh. 'I just needed to know whether Emily might know, or…'

'I would never say. But even if she did know…' He gave a casual shrug. 'It was just sex. It's hardly a crime.'

It had felt like one to her—at least afterwards it had, Anna thought as she scooped out more seriously delicious mussels from her dish.

And then it was Sebastián who had a question—or rather, an observation. 'You didn't tell your mother about the baby being born.'

'Didn't anyone ever tell you that it's rude to listen in on other people's calls?'

'No.' He shrugged again. 'And anyway, it's the only way I seem to find anything out about you—' He bit back whatever he'd been about to say next, and gave a tight smile as he referred to that awful morning.

'I didn't tell them because I don't know enough myself, and I don't want to scare Willow.'

'How old is your daughter?'

But Anna didn't answer.

She was still feeling so angry, and that wasn't

like her. She tried not to let things get to her, but on this subject she was so cross that she put down her glass and looked him right in the eyes.

'How dare you think you have the right to judge me?'

Black eyes met and held hers, and she awaited his arrogant reply as she replayed in her mind his awful words that morning.

'Anna, I apologise.' He held her gaze and nodded, as if confirming his own choice of words. 'I regret what I said that morning and my reaction.'

She could feel her teeth clenching together in her tense jaw.

'I've regretted what I said for months.'

'Oh, please…' Anna responded coldly. She was about to call for the bill, but they both knew he would have to pay for dinner, and what was more, she didn't care about manners tonight, so instead she reached for her bag and stood.

'Anna,' he said calmy, 'please sit down.'

'I don't want to,' she snapped, and was suddenly confused.

Because shouldn't an apology that sounded sincere make her feel better? Instead the anger seemed to be rising inside her.

She leaned her head closer to his and in low tones expressed exactly how much he'd hurt her. 'That was my first time away from my daughter since she was born, and I didn't tell you about her because I was tearful about leaving her. In any case, it's none of your business, and I didn't think a man like you would be particularly interested in hearing about my childcare arrangements.'

'Anna, please sit down,' he said. 'Or if you want to shout let's take this conversation outside.'

'I don't want to be outside with you,' Anna said, but she did sit back down and stared angrily across at him. 'You hurt me that morning. A lot. I was already feeling bad enough about leaving her, and you have no right to judge me.'

'How old is your daughter?'

This time she answered. 'Four...almost five.' Anna took a sip of her drink and actually felt better for saying her piece—well, almost. 'As I said, you wouldn't think twice if it was a father who left his child for a weekend.'

'No, it's not that.'

She made a soft scoffing noise with pale lips that told him she was still deeply upset. And Sebastián, who rarely explained himself, knew she deserved a better explanation.

'We got too close,' he said. 'I didn't like it. I was already planning to pull back—'

'What do you mean?'

'We got too close,' he repeated, but refused to elaborate on that particular matter. 'Then I heard you say "I love you, darling", and it sounded as if you meant it. But then you said you had a daughter...'

'Did you think gold-digger Emily's friend was just like her? After a rich daddy for her child—?'

'Anna,' he broke in, his tone short, and it halted her. 'Are you going to let me explain or not? Believe me, I'd prefer not to.'

She gave a small, tense nod, which invited him to continue when he'd really rather not, but he pushed on.

'When I heard you say "I love you", I was maybe angry…a bit jealous, even…' he admitted, and then frowned, surprised to have said that.

He never revealed such things—just didn't—but her glaring eyes were waiting, which didn't make it any easier. He took a sip of his drink and for once knew he was the uncomfortable one.

'I wasn't upset that you have a daughter. I was upset with you for leaving her.'

She frowned, parted her lips to question him, but then snapped them closed, as if consciously letting him finish. He wished now he had left the whole subject alone.

'I thought we had spent enough time together that you might have spoken about her, mentioned her… Maria left when I was about ten. Alejandro was five. Carmen not even one.'

How ironic that he now wished she would interrupt, so he could draw a line under the entire thing, but she remained silent, her green eyes more curious than angry now.

'She was away a lot even before that, though. Affairs, lovers… I didn't really understand that then, but…' He had never articulated it, not even to his family, but he had spent a lot of time alone on his yacht in recent months, thinking. 'When Carmen was maybe two years old she was sick—nothing terrible, but she had a fever. The nanny was trying to calm her and the doctor came. I remember going into the lounge. My mother was on TV, doing a live interview on a talk show. Laughing, flirting, dancing. Clearly without a care or any thought as to what was happening with her children at home.'

'Out of sight, out of mind?'

Anna repeated what he had said to her that morning, but her voice was without anger now.

'Yes.' He nodded. 'I overreacted. I don't usually.'

It was possibly the understatement of his life. In the relationship department his baseline setting was freezing cold—Sebastián knew that much about himself. His passion was reserved solely for business, and not just the family one. He had major investments of his own. Certainly he would never be reliant on any one thing or person. Yet that morning he hadn't just frostily pulled back, as he always did if anyone got too close. He'd been savage.

'I should never have said what I did. But I was already smarting from the "I love you", and then…'

'I get it.'

Anna knew none of that had been easy for him to admit.

'So can you accept my apology?' he asked.

'Yes.'

And she did. It felt odd to sit there facing him, with all the anger and hurt of these past months fading away to nothing.

'Thank you,' she nodded.

'No, thank *you*,' he said.

Clearly uncomfortable with all he'd revealed, he glanced at their empty plates in relief.

'I'll get the bill.' He went to signal to the waiter, then remembered to be polite. 'Unless you want dessert?'

Anna shook her head, but although she didn't want dessert, she also did not want the night to end just yet. He made her so curious.

'Coffee would be nice though.'

He ordered coffee for Anna, and for himself his own brand of sherry. 'Spot-check,' he said.

'To make sure they keep it in stock?'

'More to make sure that it is our sherry in the bottle.'

'That's not very trusting,' she said.

'Because I'm *not* very trusting.'

It was Romero sherry, Sebastián confirmed when their drinks had been served and he had taken a sip.

'Your mother is the dancer on the bottle's label,' Anna said. 'I remember that from when Emily was doing the website.'

'She's on the label *for now*,' Sebastián said darkly.

'And your parents are back together?'

'Yes,' he nodded. 'She has wheedled her way back in since my father became ill. The wedding was their first public outing, to show off their reconciliation.'

She could better see now why he had rushed to judgement that morning.

'How is it?' Anna asked. 'Now that your mother is back?'

'We call her Maria,' he said.

'So how is it now that Maria's back?'

He gave her a brief smile, like a little reward for her persistence. 'My preference would be to have nothing to do with her. But for now, for the sake of my father, I am courteous.'

'For now?'

'I'll cut her loose when my father dies,' Sebastián said. 'I'll completely erase her from the brand.'

The cold steel in his voice sent goosebumps up her arms and served as another reminder, as if she had needed it, that this man severed ties easily.

'What about your brother and sister? Do they feel as strongly as you?'

He pondered the question for a moment. 'No. Alejandro sees both sides. Carmen loathes her and refuses to hide it. I can't blame her.' He swirled his drink and then met her eyes. 'I am concerned for Carmen.'

'Why?'

'Just am.' He shrugged, as if realising he had once again been too open, and then changed the topic. 'Enjoy the peace while it lasts,' he suggested, then drained his drink. 'The circus is coming to town.'

They wandered slowly back to their villas. The pink had gone from the sky and it was now a vivid navy expanse, with a strip of aqua where it met the horizon and stars were sparkling up high. Music was throbbing and Puerto Banús was far from sleepy, with lots of people milling about. He took her arm at one point, as a flashy car screeched down an impossibly narrow street.

Anna liked the feel of his hand on her arm and was suddenly confused.

She really had forgiven him.

The hurt she had been carrying had gone.

For months she'd looked at that incredible night through pained eyes, and yet now the sky might just as well still be pink, because she felt her rose-tinted glasses snap back on.

The time they had shared was not tainted now, although she forced herself to recall how he had hurt Emily in the past, as well his callously discarded fiancée, and how this man planned to cut off his mother without a backward glance.

'Thank you for dinner,' she said as they reached her villa.

'You're welcome,' he said.

'Text me if you hear anything from the hospital.'

'Of course… Anna?'

'Yes?'

But his mouth pressed together, perhaps changing his mind about whatever he'd been about to say, and then he shook his head, denying her the elaboration of his thoughts. Yet there was something about his silence that weakened her resolve. Something about this man that had her wanting to throw caution aside. *Again*.

The palm trees were rustling above them, and the same breeze blew her hair across her face. Anna brushed it back and met his eyes.

'I wanted to do that,' he admitted, looking at her hair.

She'd wanted him to as well. Had wanted him to smooth her hair back behind her ear and stroke his way to the kiss that had been waiting in the air. But he'd made no move.

He broke the tense silence by explaining, 'But I know I shouldn't mess up my apology.'

There was a subtle offer there, and Anna heard it. It was for her to decide if they would resume what they had started at the wedding.

But she couldn't. She just couldn't.

'Goodnight, Sebastián.'

'Sleep well.'

She let herself into the villa and stood for a moment with her back to the door, resisting the urge to change her mind, reminding herself of what Sebastián himself had said earlier.

'It was just sex.'

Only for Anna it didn't feel quite as simple as that.

There was nothing casual about her feelings.

She liked Sebastián Romero way more than could be considered wise.

CHAPTER SEVEN

ANNA WAS INCREDIBLY tempted to skip breakfast, but decided she would not hide from Sebastián and headed to the restaurant.

After selecting white shorts and a pretty cheese-cloth top, she pulled on sandals and then strolled through the gorgeous grounds.

'*Señorita...*'

She was greeted warmly and taken to a terrace table overlooking the delicious ocean, where she gave her order for coffee. Having chosen some fruit and yoghurt from the splendid buffet, Anna was just starting to relax when the apologetic waiter came over.

'*Señorita*, please forgive me...but we have a group of guests and they would like privacy on the terrace.'

She glanced up and saw that two couples had arrived. While privately wondering why they couldn't sit at any one of the many vacant tables, not wanting to make a fuss, she stood up, and was about to be shown to one of the tables inside when Sebastián appeared. He looked seedy—unshaven and with bloodshot eyes. Still, even at his most ragged, he was easily the best-looking man she had ever met.

'What's going on?' he asked.

'There's a group,' Anna said. 'I think they want to close off the terrace for them.'

'*Perdóneme?*' he said, and frowned at the waiter who, under Sebastián's steely gaze, looked rather less authoritative as he explained in Spanish the reason for the table-change.

Sebastián answered in English. 'I don't give a damn. If they require a degree of privacy then they'll have to wait—or they can eat in their own rooms.' He looked over to her. 'Sit down, Anna.'

'It's really no problem…'

'Well, it is for me,' he said. 'I like the view.'

He took a seat, and Anna did the same.

'I really don't mind moving.'

'Well, I do.'

He ordered coffee and she watched him yawn. She guessed he hadn't returned to his villa after leaving her.

'I was just about to text Emily,' she told him. 'I didn't want to disturb her too early.'

'No need. I have just come from breakfast with Alejandro.'

Gosh, Anna thought, he certainly got things done.

'The baby is doing well for its dates and size. Though I forgot to ask what it weighed again. Emily is…' he rolled his hand '…emotional.'

'With good reason.'

'I'm not criticising,' Sebastián said. 'Just report-ing.' He met her eyes and gave her a small smile. 'What else…?' He thought for a moment. 'She's asked if you will get her a few things. There's quite a list.'

He took out his phone to read from his list, and Anna took out hers so she could type the list into her Notes app. Then he suggested he just send her the list instead.

'Okay, but let's go through it so I can get her exactly what she wants.'

'Lip gloss.'

'Lip gloss?' she checked. 'Oh, do you mean lip balm?'

'I took it to be lip gloss.' He looked at her mouth, and then back to her eyes. He could flirt like a pro, with a single glance. With a single word. 'Maybe balm.'

There was no balm to be had in his gaze, so she flicked her eyes away and got back to the list.

It was quite extensive, given Emily had left Jerez with no notice, having expected to have three more months left to prepare herself for the arrival of her baby.

'I'll drive you to the hospital once you've got the shopping,' Sebastián told her.

'I can get a taxi.'

'If you prefer,' he said. 'Carmen is arriving tomorrow.'

'What about your parents?'

'My father has a hospital appointment in Madrid later in the week. I told him things were stable enough here, and that he should keep his appointment and then come afterwards.'

'You've been busy.'

'I've barely started,' he said. 'I'll head back to Jerez soon. With Alejandro now on paternity leave, one of us has to work.'

'But I thought your yacht was…arriving?'

Or whatever the correct term was!

He nodded. 'I might tell Alejandro he can use it. They'll be good to him.'

'They?'

'My crew,' he said. 'They're like family, really.'

'Oh…' She frowned, because this really was another world to her. 'So, does it just follow you around?'

'No!' He gave a half-laugh. 'It has been out on charter, but that's just finished and they had already started preparing the yacht for me. I was going to take a break before Alejandro took time off for the new baby.'

'So you lease it out? I mean, charter it?'

'Not often—and only to friends or associates. But I have a crew who love to travel and be on the water,' Sebastián explained.

Perhaps he registered her frown.

'So do I,' he said, 'although it's more than that.'

'In what way?'

'It's something to share,' he said.

'For parties?'

'At times—though not of late.' He thought for a

moment. 'It is nice for family gatherings and such. Special times. You might see it for yourself. The crew are already planning a celebration for my new niece.'

'That's nice.'

'They are far more thoughtful than I am,' he admitted. 'I have an apartment outside of Jerez, near the port. I really can't imagine having such gatherings there, nor in a hotel or function room. The yacht is different.'

'How?'

'It's home,' he said, 'with an incredible crew. They know my family. Believe me, that helps. My family is a lot to deal with...'

'I'd have loved to have a big family...' Anna sighed wistfully. 'I'd love brothers and sisters for Willow too.'

'You want more children?'

He pulled a face, looking so incredulous that it made her laugh.

'You really don't want a family?'

He shook his head. 'To my father's eternal dismay.' He rolled those black eyes. 'But I have a great life, and I don't want to complicate it.'

'What about when you're old?'

'I'll be old on my yacht,' he said, and gave her a smile. 'Don't worry. I'm too rich to be lonely.' He drained his coffee. 'I should go.'

'Should you drive back today?'

'Pardon?'

'Well, you've hardly slept.'

'Anna, we were in separate beds by midnight.' Then he added. '*Your* choice.'

'I meant…'

She flushed, because she knew she'd been caught fishing for information, and because she knew just how relieved she was that he *had* been in bed by midnight. But she didn't want him to go, Anna realised. She was inventing excuses for him not to leave.

It was just so nice to be like this with him. Even with the annoying background of their fellow diners, one of whom was now complaining that the sun was too bright.

'No doubt she finds the water too blue,' Sebastián muttered, and then said something entirely unexpected. 'I was once engaged to a woman like that.'

He gave himself a little shake. She couldn't tell if it was because he was surprised that he'd said it, or to rid himself of the memory of this woman.

'What happened?' Anna asked, unable to help herself. 'With your fiancée?'

'Plenty.'

'It must have hurt, though?' she ventured. 'When it ended?'

'Yes.'

'Did you love her?'

'No.'

Now it was Anna who gave a slightly disparaging laugh. 'That would do it...'

'Believe me, it was never about love.' He looked over at her. 'On either side.' Perhaps he saw the slight twist of her mouth, because he added, 'Whatever you might have read.'

Anna flushed. 'I'm not usually so nosey. I just—'

'It's fine.' He gave a small shrug, as if forgiving her for her brief foray into internet stalking. 'I certainly looked *you* up after we...'

'What did you find out?'

'Nothing,' he admitted. 'I found your parents. Oh, and a photo of them, the proud grandparents, in one of your father's parish newsletters.' Now he gave her a smile. 'Your daughter was dressed as a unicorn.'

'Oh, that was so last year!' Anna laughed. 'She's into flamenco dancing now. Emily brought her back this dreadful dress—'

She halted, suddenly worried about disparaging his heritage—especially given his mother was a famous flamenco dancer.

'It's bright green with black polka dots...' she attempted, trying to explain the fright of this dress. 'I'm sure most are gorgeous, but this one...'

Her voice trailed off as he started scrolling through his phone, but she knew she must forgive him. Because what would he know about four-year-olds who wanted to wear their flamenco dresses to the shops, to school, to church, to bed...? As well as that, he was clearly up to his eyeballs in putting out Romero fires, with the family planning to descend on Marbella at any moment.

Despite his little jab about separate beds, Sebastián was mightily relieved that they hadn't slept together last night.

She'd opened up his heart when he preferred to keep it closed.

'Do you want a lift to the hospital later?' he offered, one last time.

'If it's not too inconvenient.'

He nodded, and went to go, but then changed his mind. 'You are beyond an inconvenience, Anna Douglas.'

If she told anyone else what he'd said, or if she attempted to repeat it, it would sound like an insult or a criticism.

You probably had to be looking into his bloodshot black eyes to really interpret his meaning, Anna thought. Or you had to be inhaling the dregs of last night's cologne over the breakfast table to understand.

Because inconvenient was exactly what this attraction was.

Their attraction was so intense, so *present*, that it shocked her. She thought of his mild invitation last night and knew she could not be this playboy's occasional fling.

He would move on—that much he had told her.

One night had been a delicious oddity.

Two might break her...

'As are you,' Anna replied now, staring back at this man she would prefer not to want to quite this degree.

And with that, he got up and left.

She sat alone at the table, but without him she felt uncomfortable. And as she went to choose from the gorgeous pastry selection she knew why.

'Not so bold without your boss here.'

Anna turned. It was one of the women in the group for whom Sebastián had refused to move. She must have seen them both with their phones out and assumed that Anna worked for him. And she hadn't finished with her snide digs yet.

'And I thought the Romero brand was about elegance...'

And, no, here in Puerto Banús Anna found she *wasn't* so bold without Sebastián there.

She sat back down at her table for a few moments, trying to eat the pastry she had selected. Then she pretended to use her phone, just for something to do. But she could feel the ice of the woman's gaze upon her and soon left.

Sebastián drove her to the hospital, but declined to come inside.

'Alejandro is going to sit with the baby while

you visit Emily.' He looked over at her. 'What are you going to do this afternoon?'

'I'm not sure. I'll go to the beach, maybe—see if I can go home with a tan.'

'Don't burn like a tourist. Take it slow.'

'I'm not going to get burnt.'

'Okay,' he said, in a voice that meant business. 'Now I'm going to ask the awkward question: Do you need some money?'

'No!'

'Because it is expensive here. Use the restaurant at the hotel, and room service, and when you're on the beach just charge everything to the villa.' He must have seen her eyes close. 'But you won't do that, will you?'

'I'll get some snacks at the shop to take with me.'

'Dios!' He had the audacity to laugh. 'Just—' Then he must have seen her pained face. 'Go and see your friend.'

Sebastián watched her walk off, her pale legs poking out of her ill-fitting white shorts, and he thought of her on the extremely exclusive beach, unpacking a lunch box while burning alive and being roasted by the rest of the clientele.

He did not want to get involved with Anna, but he was very aware that he'd messed up her first weekend away from her daughter.

And now circumstance was ruining Anna's first holiday without her.

Instead of relaxing, she was stuck with hospital visits.

Instead of spending time with her friend, Anna was alone.

His apology wasn't enough, Sebastián knew. He wanted to make up for that morning.

The hospital was cool—until she stepped onto the maternity ward, which was so hot Anna felt as if she might already be on the beach.

Having washed her hands, she was shown to a gorgeous room and there, looking tearful and utterly exhausted, was Emily.

'This wasn't how it was supposed to be!' Emily blurted out and promptly burst into tears.

'Oh, you poor thing!' Anna gave her a hug. 'I'm so glad I'm here…even if I can't see you very much. How is she?'

'They say she's doing well…' Emily gulped. 'But they're having to help her with her breathing. There are so many machines…'

There were indeed a lot of machines, Anna thought as they gazed through the glass at the special care unit.

Oh, gosh, she was so tiny, and yet so perfect. The hair poking out of her little knitted hat grew in blonde tufts, like Emily's, and her tiny hands were pink and reaching out, as if trying to hold on to something.

And there was Alejandro, his hand going into

the porthole and taking his tiny daughter's fingers, utterly engrossed, at first unaware of his audience. Then he saw them and gave Anna a smile, pointing to the cap and gown he was wearing.

It's fine, Anna mouthed, and then put her fingers into the sign of a heart and pointed to their daughter.

'I feel dreadful that you're here alone,' Emily said when they were back in her suite.

'I'm fine. Sebastián's been great.'

'Oh, please…' Emily disparaged as she gingerly got back into bed. 'Alejandro asked him to take care of you and he's already belting back to Jerez to work. Did he give you my list?'

'He did,' Anna said, ever practical, and handed over what felt like half the contents of the *farmacia* she had been to, as well as the items of clothing Emily had asked for. 'And I made this…'

Anna passed Emily the tissue paper package and held her breath as she opened it carefully.

'Oh, Anna!'

'I'm not sure there's much call for cashmere blankets during a Spanish summer…'

She laughed, trying to make light of the gift. She had embroidered two otters, one dark and one pale, onto a mocha background, and stitched them onto a backing so both sides would be soft.

'It's perfect…' Emily was tearful again, but in a good way. 'Remember those otters at the lake?'

'Willow adores them. I'm sure our girls are going to have lots of fun watching them together.'

'I hope so.'

'I *know* so,' Anna said. 'Your daughter is beautiful. And, yes, she's early, but everyone seems very positive.'

'Yes…' Emily took a breath and gazed at the blanket. 'This is gorgeous, Anna.' She looked lovingly up at her friend and asked, 'Would it be a lot of work to add her name?'

'I can take it back home with me and do it.'

'I mean, while you're here.'

'I can't embroider a name I don't know,' Anna said, keeping her voice light while thinking of the mountain of work it would be to get it done in time. Not so much the embroidery, it was more restitching the backing without her trusty sewing machine. As well as that, the boutiques she'd seen here so far didn't really look as if they would sell the type of silk thread she required.

'Is it doable, though?'

'Of course!' Anna forced a positive tone, but it changed to one of pure delight when Emily confided the baby's name. 'That's beautiful.'

'It's top secret.'

In all, it was a lovely visit, and Anna stayed for a couple of hours, watching as glorious pink flowers and balloons were delivered, until Emily headed off for some time with her baby.

'I'll be back tomorrow,' Anna said, and hugged her friend.

'Well, hopefully I'll be better company. All I seem to do at the moment is cry.'

'Please!' Anna dismissed her concerns. 'Remember when I had Willow? I was hardly swinging from the rafters.'

'You didn't cry at the drop of a hat.'

No, she had just been silent.

She had been hurting for the tiny baby that its father didn't deign to visit. And so angry that her parents could consider her precious child a mistake.

No streams of pink flowers and *It's a girl!* balloons had arrived for her. And Anna's only visitor had been Emily.

As she took the lift to the ground floor, Anna tried to work out where she might find sewing supplies in Marbella. She did some searching on her phone, but couldn't find anything that looked promising. She knew Emily wasn't thinking clearly, but Anna didn't really want to be sewing on her holiday…

Stepping out from the cool air-conditioned hospital into the fierce midday sun felt like opening an oven door.

'Anna!'

She looked towards the source of her name being called and there he was, leaning against his car, shaved now, dressed in a dark suit and tie and wearing shades.

'I thought you were heading back to Jerez?' Anna said as she walked over.

'Maybe you are right and I am too tired to drive.' He shrugged. 'I worked online this morning instead.'

His car was like a delicious fridge as she climbed in.

'So, what are your plans?' he asked, and glanced over at her.

'I need to get a couple of things, so I might go into the old town.'

'Or we could go to the beach?'

'No, thank you.'

'You don't want to go to the beach?'

She took a breath and looked out at the gorgeous sand and sparkling waters. Of course she wanted to go to the beach. But she felt weak at the thought of an afternoon with him.

She recognised the danger of it…felt that pit-of-the-stomach recklessness she hadn't known existed until she had spent the night with him.

It would not be repeated.

But…

It was just a trip to the beach…maybe a swim.

In the middle of the day.

An afternoon in the delicious sun with him was more than she knew how to refuse.

'Yes,' Anna said, as if it were a simple decision. 'Actually, that would be lovely.'

CHAPTER EIGHT

ANNA WOULD *NOT* BURN.

She had a pump bottle of the same lotion that she used on Willow, and she slathered it on in her room, and even put it in her bag for repeat applications.

The butterflies were back as she tied on her red bikini and wrapped her pale body in the sarong, then added a straw hat. Then she headed down the path he had pointed to last night.

'Hola!' he said when he opened the door, wearing black swimming trunks and sunglasses, completely at ease in his own skin. 'Come through.'

'I thought we were going to the beach.'

He pointed behind him and she blinked at the sight of his bedroom and a to-die-for view of the sea.

'Wow!' she said. 'I'm going to put in a complaint about my accommodation.'

He smiled at her little joke as they walked across the cool marble floor and then through his huge bedroom and straight out onto the beach.

It was only when they arrived and she saw a couple of bronzed topless women glance over that she felt overdressed. The red and white sarong that had looked so pretty before now felt as if she'd draped herself in an English flag.

'Here,' Sebastián said, and flopped down on one of the sun loungers.

'You've given me the shaded one.'

'You *need* the shaded one,' he said. 'Or you'll burn.'

'No...' She looked up from under the brim of her hat. 'I have impenetrable sunblock on.'

She looked tense, Sebastián thought as he took off his sunglasses and placed them on the small table between them. Usually he didn't babysit anyone. He was more used to handing over his credit card and leaving his chosen date to amuse herself while he got on with work.

What was he doing here? Sebastián questioned.

He felt...*duty-bound* to stay and ensure that Anna was okay and could navigate the politics of the beach...

No, not duty-bound.

This wasn't duty.

'*Dios*...' he muttered as the awful group from that morning paraded past to their reserved loungers. 'This is why I prefer my yacht.'

Sebastian turned his head and gave her a lazy smile that told her he didn't mind at all being there.

'She thinks I work for you.' The words slipped out before she could stop herself.

'How do you know that?'

'Just a comment she made at breakfast, after you left.' Her lips pinched and she shook her head, not wanting to repeat it. But there was a certain patience in his silence, a space in the pause that encouraged honesty. 'She suggested the Romeros were lowering their standards of elegance by employing me.'

'*She* is the one who lowers things,' Sebastián said. 'Watch! She'll start complaining before she even lies down.'

Anna looked over and, sure enough, she already had the beach boys moving umbrellas and was generating unnecessary fuss on this beautiful day. Thankfully she hadn't spotted Anna, and hopefully wouldn't. Still, it did nothing to allay her tension as she lay there.

'Was your fiancée really like that?' she ventured, wondering if he'd warn her not to ask, but he didn't seem to mind.

'Not at first...' He yawned before continuing, 'But then I heard she had reprimanded one my crew.' He looked over at Anna. 'It's protocol that the *capitán* deals with such issues.'

'So, she should have gone through the captain?'

'No, she should have gone through me, and I would have spoken to Dante.'

'Your captain?'

'Yes. But in this instance there was no reason for her to complain. She was just being a bitch.'

'Don't swear.'

'Believe me, she would make a saint curse. I guess that was my first glimpse into the real her.

I can usually spot her type a mile off, but Ella hid it well, I'll give her that.'

Anna forgot all about their horrible beach companion as she turned and looked at him, desperate for him to elaborate further, but he didn't.

'What really happened?' she asked.

He put his hands behind his head and said nothing.

'I don't believe you'd break things off just like that.'

'Anna, I *do* break things off just like that,' Sebastián refuted. 'Often.'

It wasn't an easy, companionable conversation. There were lots of long silences, during which they listened to the lulling, shushing waves between question and answer.

'Not if you're engaged to someone.' Anna just wouldn't buy it. 'Not when she's just lost a baby. I don't believe it.' She saw him blink, but had no idea what that blink meant. It just felt to her as if she'd hit on the truth. 'I don't believe you'd do that.'

He closed his eyes then, and for a little while Anna assumed he'd fallen asleep, but finally she heard his voice.

'I promised Ella I would never discuss it.'

'Did she agree the same?'

He gave a curt nod.

'Then why do you come off so badly in all her interviews? I don't see *her* maintaining a dignified silence.'

'Maybe not. But it's not always about setting the record straight. Perhaps there are things that are just too…' He halted. 'I don't care what people think of me.'

But as she lay there, wishing she had a scrap of his confidence, Sebastián spoke again.

'Most of the time.'

Anna turned her head and found she was holding her breath as she met his eyes.

'I'm not going to go into details,' Sebastián said, 'but the rumours are not true.'

She nodded, and in a place deep inside she knew she was being told the truth. Her cheeks were stinging as he subtly told her that her opinion of him mattered.

'I wish I didn't care what people thought,' Anna admitted.

'Why do you?'

'I think because my parents do. I grew up being told that everything I did reflected on them. It's quite a small village where I'm from, so everyone knows everything.'

'Do you work?'

'Of course I work,' Anna said. 'I'm a receptionist at the junior school.' She looked over at him. 'It wasn't what I planned, but…' She shrugged. 'I get school holidays off, and that's going to come in very handy.'

'What *did* you plan?'

'I wanted to be an English teacher. I'm hoping

to go back to college next year, once Willow is at school. There are a lot of supervised teaching days, though.'

She saw him frown.

'Do you get paid for that?'

'No, or I'd have done it already.'

'*I'll* supervise you.'

'I don't think it works like that!' Anna laughed.

She found herself pinking up, and not from the sun, and she looked at him, wondering how he could make even the most casual conversation a decadent flirtation.

'You're starting to burn,' Sebastián said, and Anna chose not to tell him that she was simply blushing.

He took her giant-sized, industrial strength sunblock from the top of her bag.

'Next time just bring a small tube.'

'Why?'

'Because you're not on a school field trip!'

He was trying to tell her gently how things were done here. He was trying to explain the world he had landed her in, which could at times be catty, but he saw her lips pinch and knew she felt criticised.

'Hold out your hand.'

She did so, and he pumped a generous dollop onto her palm. 'Left shoulder.' He watched as she rubbed it in. 'And left side of your neck.'

A beach waiter came and Sebastián ordered iced

water and lime for himself. Then the waiter glanced to Anna.

'I've got mine, thanks.'

Sebastián looked at her plastic water bottle, practically coming to a boil in the sun, and changed his order.

'Two iced waters with lime, and a plate of fruit.' As the waiter walked off, he interrupted her before she could protest. 'You can save your hot water for emergencies.'

'Why are you so arrogant?'

'I'm really not.'

'Oh, you really are,' Anna said, and rolled over.

She tried to focus on her book, the same gritty biography she'd attempted to read on the plane—but it was impossible to get through a single paragraph with the presence of the demi-god by her side.

Their water came, and it was icy and delicious and served with the most gorgeous fruit platter she had ever seen.

'Have some,' he said as he bit into a slice of bright pink watermelon that had Anna's mouth watering.

But although tempted, she knew there was sand and unabsorbed sunblock on her fingers.

'No, thank you.'

She went back to her book, but still couldn't concentrate. She was just so impossibly aware of the man next to her and trying hard not to reveal it.

'Why are we fighting over fruit and water?' he asked, and she looked over.

'And sunblock,' she added curtly.

'Yes, and sunblock,' he snapped back. 'Seriously, Anna, I get that you would prefer not to be here in Puerto Banús—'

'It's not that!'

'Okay. Then I get that it's awkward for you. But please—let it go. It's a glass of water.'

'It's not the water.'

'Then what? Didn't I apologise adequately?'

She closed her eyes and let out a huff of frustration.

'Because we are still fighting and I don't get why.'

'I'm not fighting.'

'You are.'

She stared at the blurred words on the page of her book and knew he was right.

She was fighting their attraction—playing some odd whack-a-mole game with her senses.

And now Sebastián thought she was being petty by not eating the fruit that of course she wanted...

She sat up and tried to pretend that the man beside her didn't affect her, but she saw the gorgeous hair on his thighs, and knew how they felt against hers... She tried to squash down that memory.

He saw she was eating and sat up.

'Good,' he said, as if pleased their silent fight was over.

As she reached for a slice of chilled pineapple her hand hovered as she saw the opened passion fruit and the little spoons beside it, and the mixture of thinly sliced crisp green and ruby-red apples.

She watched his confident fingers move to pluck a ripe strawberry, and it was then that she spoke, her voice breathy and bewildered. 'I'm very happy to be here.'

His olive-skinned fingers hesitated, and she watched as they took the tips of hers before he spoke. 'Good.'

She looked at their hands, lightly touching. The contact stirred the energy trapped somewhere within her, drawing it out of her, yet at the same time returning it and matching his... It was like a circuit connecting.

'*Are* we fighting?' she asked, honestly unsure.

'You are,' he said, and dropped the contact, taking up his strawberry and lying back against the headrest. 'But it is not a fight of anger. Not any more.'

She looked at him and he stared back boldly, his black eyes telling her that the next move was hers. How badly she wanted to reach over and take his hand again! How much every cell in her body wanted to let him pull her towards him, to kiss him, to stroke him!

His bed was a mere few steps away...

'I'm going in the water,' Anna said abruptly as she stood.

Perhaps in the water she could breathe and cool her heated thoughts. She would welcome the return of her common sense.

Sebastián put his hands behind his head and watched her walk towards the ocean. He saw that her shoulders were pink, and although he admired the curve of her buttocks, and the length of her thighs, it was her gorgeous back that he prized... the tension in her straight spine...

As idyllic as the beach appeared, the clientele on such exclusive resorts were not always kind—especially if they felt that they had been slighted.

He heard the woman from this morning make a comment about cheap high street bikinis and pink skin that burned, and laugh at how the English girl would suffer for lying in the sun tonight...

It was all said in Spanish, however, the mocking tone was understood universally, and the derisive laughter from the group evident.

He saw Anna's shoulders stiffen, her stride briefly hesitate, and he held his breath.

Yes, Anna had hesitated—because being laughed at on the beach told her what she already knew: she didn't belong here.

She understood now that he *was* supervising her. Kindly, but still...

From the sunblock to the water and fruit, he

was trying to help her blend in, in this rather cruel world.

She resumed walking towards the water, even though she wanted to turn and run.

'Anna!'

His voice reached her and the panic stilled.

'Wait for me.'

Anna turned and watched as he walked towards her, taking in his sheer beauty. She noted that the mocking laughter had faded into incredulous silence, because he'd grasped her hand to walk with her, and then he gave her a kiss that told all present how beautiful he found her.

It was a light kiss, an easy kiss, and even though it was delivered for the purpose of annoying her detractors, Anna revelled in it.

It made her feel beautiful.

As they walked hand in hand into the water she felt as perfect and whole as she had that night in his arms.

But the water, Anna realised, could never have shocked common sense into her. Because instead of the cold seas she was familiar with, this one was warm bliss—there wasn't even a yelp as the ocean met her stomach.

'Thank you,' she said.

'For what?'

'I don't know exactly what they said…' She looked at him. 'But you didn't have to do that, you know.'

'I wanted to,' he responded. 'Actually, I would like to do a whole lot more…'

And with that he swam off, far more expertly than her school swimming lessons would allow her to do, so instead she lay back and let the ocean support her.

The sky was the bluest she had ever seen, and the sun by far too bright to look directly at. So she squinted, and through her lashes saw the golden fire and its haze shining down on her. And then it was blocked out by the figure of Sebastián Romero. He stood there, dripping wet and looking down at her.

It was more dangerous to look directly at him than at the sun, she thought.

Yet she did.

And she floated there, recalling another time when he had looked down on her, and she knew he was remembering the same.

'Please don't…' she said.

'Don't what?'

'Don't look at me like that.'

It was odd to say it out loud. She felt uncomfortable addressing openly the warm flood of feelings his look had generated.

'As if we might…'

'Might…?' he checked, offering his hand and saving her from inelegantly trying to stand up on the sandy bottom.

He did not remove his hand.

The sand was soft, yet firm beneath her feet, the water waist-high, and his gaze drifted down her pinkening body, eventually coming to rest on the nipples that poked against her flimsy bikini.

He touched her neck where the skin was pink, and the shoulder that she must have missed with the sunblock.

'We could go back inside,' he said, and his low, throaty voice told her it was not simply to save her from burning that he made the suggestion.

Right now, standing barely dressed and facing each other, felt challenging enough to Anna.

She was unused to wanting. Naively, she'd thought that night-time was the danger zone—that walking back from dinner would be when her resolve might weaken.

When she'd said yes to the beach, it had been because surely it would be easier to keep her head at midday?

'You should stop that,' he said, as he caressed her cheek.

'Stop what?'

'Looking at me as if you want me to kiss you.'

She wanted to retort quickly, *In your dreams*. But she did not. She could feel his fingers in her hair, smoothing it back from her face as he'd wanted to last night, then sliding to the back of her head to grasp the silken strands more firmly. The sun beat down on them, and on the glistening water, and there was no place to hide.

So she stared back at him instead, and when his face came down towards hers, she closed her eyes in utter bliss at the feel of his mouth, soft and firm and capable of making her shiver on a blazing day… Her hands went to his shoulders, to the warm sun-heated skin there. She liked the noises they made as they kissed, and how hot their skin felt where it touched. Then his hand moved down to her waist, and only then did she pull back.

'I don't think…' She was trying to be honest, to thrash out a deal with the devil while there was still a chance. 'This can't go anywhere…'

'Agreed,' Sebastián said.

Clearly he did not make promises he had no intention of keeping, and she could only admire him for that.

'You don't want a relationship and…' she took a breath '… I'm in no position to have one.'

'Yes.'

'So, why would we…?'

'Because we want each other.'

She couldn't deny that truth.

'Because we can,' he said.

And his hand moved from her waist up to her ribcage, as it had when they'd danced. He stroked her gently, but not in a calming way.

'I don't want anyone finding out,' she said.

'I'm sure we're not anyone's priority,' he said. 'We don't have to hide.'

'No!'

She was adamant. He confused every principle she held, and all her thought processes, but she was clear on this. They stood in the water, hearing the laughter and the sounds of summer around them.

'I will always be friends with Emily, and I don't want anything awkward—'

'Why would it be awkward just because we've had sex?'

And therein lay the difference between them—and Anna knew it.

Sex was sex to him. A need. A want fulfilled.

She was deliciously crazy about him and wishing it *could* just be sex...wishing that his kiss moved only her body and not her soul as well.

'Next time I'm here it will be with my daughter.' She held firm. 'I don't want there to be even a hint that you're anything more to me than my best friend's husband's brother.'

'Believe me,' he said, 'if you are here with your child I will be staying well back. I don't do relationships, and certainly not complicated ones. Stop making something simple so involved.'

He kissed her again, his mouth soothing the doubts—or was he just inflaming her desire, so that there was no room for anything other than the lust that rippled through her?

'Let's go back to the villa...'

Their foreheads were touching, their bodies barely an inch apart, but she prickled in a way that told her they very soon would be skin to skin.

Anna wanted to take his hand and go to the delicious places he promised, but she attempted one last stab at reason.

'I don't want Emily to—'

'How could she know?' He attempted to reassure her. 'I go back to Jerez tomorrow.'

She felt as if the water surged beneath her as disappointment that he was leaving tomorrow hit like an invisible wave in beautiful, calm water. The shock of his words was enough to make Anna see sense.

'I can't…' She peeled herself away from him. 'I thought we had all week.'

'Anna, my brother can't work because of the baby…nor can my father because he is unwell. Carmen certainly doesn't do anything at the bodega, so someone has to be there.'

'Of course.' Logically she understood that, but her brain was pointing out that one night…or six… it didn't really matter. It was a very temporary arrangement whichever way she looked at it…

But she'd done that before, Anna realised, and she did not want the rest of her time here to be spent getting over him. Did not want to be pulled in further for only a fleeting time.

He thought she was the woman he'd met at the wedding, the persona she'd stepped into, but she was back in her own skin now.

Or halfway between the two…

'I can't,' she said, then repeated it more firmly. 'I

can't be yours again just for a night. It's not enough.
I want a holiday at least.'

She could justify that in her mind, Anna felt. A
holiday romance, but not just sex.

It was more than that already, though. Standing
in the gorgeous water, lying on the loungers, eating
together… For her, at least, if not for him.

'A holiday,' she stated again.

'That's quite a demand.'

'Oh, please,' she mocked. 'Your *life's* a holiday.'

'You really think so?'

She took a breath and looked back at him. She
knew how hard he worked, so she wasn't sure why
she had said that.

He worked hard for his family—that much she
knew too. They wouldn't be here if that wasn't the
case.

'No,' she admitted. 'I don't think that. So why
not take some time…?'

'It's impossible.'

'And another one-night stand with you is impossible for me.'

'I regret that.'

He didn't push. Instead he removed that beam
of his attention in a way she couldn't quite define.

He still held her hand as they walked out of the
water, and as she wrapped herself in her sarong
there was no impatience from him. In fact, he was
so polite that he even offered to prolong the day
with a very late lunch.

'It's almost three,' she pointed out, smiling despite already missing the sensation of being the focus of his desire, and knowing the indefinable promise of tonight that had thrummed between them had, upon her request, been removed.

'That is lunchtime in Spain.'

'Oh, well…no, thank you. I have to go to the shops and find something for Emily. I might try Old Marbella.'

'Of course.' He nodded. 'I should do some work, anyway.' He pointed to a path. 'That takes you back to your villa.'

Only lovers got to use the bedroom route, it would seem.

Still, they parted amicably, though he didn't suggest dinner. Instead, he told her she was welcome to call Reception for a driver to take her wherever she wanted to go.

He was not, Anna guessed, going to provide extended handholding for his brother's wife's friend if he was not going to get to sleep with her again. Sebastián had found her gorgeous accommodation, had taken her to dinner the first night, had driven her to and from the hospital, had even taken her to the beach, offered to do lunch…but now there was an end to it.

'Hasta luego,' he said.

Duty done.

And she only had herself to blame.

CHAPTER NINE

ANNA WOKE TO REGRET.

It was a different kind of regret, though.

She hadn't been woken with a kiss.

Nor by her sexy lover carrying a tray bearing breakfast in bed—or however this morning might have been had she given in to another night with him...

Instead, she woke alone, in gorgeous surroundings, and wished she'd been brave enough to say yes to Sebastián.

After they'd parted yesterday she had showered and pulled on new shorts and a top and wandered around Old Marbella. She'd found an odd shop tucked away that sold silk threads for her embroidery and cotton to re-stitch the backing of the blanket.

Then she'd found a café where they'd *still* been serving lunch. She'd sat under an umbrella at a table in gorgeous Orange Square, the very heart of the old town, and had ordered what she'd thought was a steak sandwich and a beer, because that had sounded very normal.

Nothing felt normal, though, she'd thought as she'd sipped on the tall, cool glass of beer and tried to tell herself that she was proud for resisting his charms.

But Anna had known she lied.

'Your veal,' the waitress had said, putting down

her plate. *'Buen provecho!'* Which Anna knew meant *Enjoy your meal*.

She would never have eaten veal at home. Not just because she couldn't afford it, but it was the principle of the thing.

And yet it would seem veal had been ordered and served, so what was she to have done?

It had been delicious!

And it was her principles that had kept her alone in her villa last night, embroidering and sewing the blanket when she could have been making reckless love.

Yes, she regretted it—especially now, when she heard a knock at the door and opened it to the stunning sight of him in a deep navy suit, but no tie, looking too sexy for words.

Clearly he was about to head for Jerez.

'Do you want to get something to eat?' he offered. 'Before I go back?'

'I'm fine,' Anna said, closing the door a little to block the view of her sewing that was laid out on the floor.

'You don't want to go to the restaurant, do you?'

'Not particularly,' Anna admitted.

'Then we can go to the marina instead.'

'Sebastián, please.' She took a breath. 'It's hard enough as it is.'

Sebastián looked at this difficult, proud woman, shutting herself away on a bright sunny day, and wondered how to make this right.

People here could be shallow sometimes, and he loathed how she'd been treated yesterday.

He thought of a way to fix things.

Of course one that might benefit him too.

'I need a favour,' he said.

'Ask away.'

'Are you going to let me in?'

'I honestly can't…'

Anna closed her eyes and knew she must sound ridiculous. 'Wait there.'

She left him at the door and hurriedly cleared the blanket she was amending away, then headed back to let him in.

'Sorry about that…'

'It's no problem.'

He came into the lounge and looked at the iced tea by the chair. He must have guessed that was where she had been sitting, so he took a seat on the sofa.

'I need a feminine perspective,' he said.

'Oh?'

'Carmen is visiting, and I am concerned about her.'

Anna saw he didn't halt himself before continuing this time.

'She has been low these past months. I know she broke up with a guy a few months ago…'

'I remember Emily saying.'

'I think it was nasty—not that she would tell me

the details,' he admitted. 'It also coincided with Maria's return.'

'Ouch.' Anna felt a touch guilty, as she'd considered Carmen simply petulant and spoilt.

'I've put it down to that, as well as our father being ill, but there's something I'm missing—something she's not telling me. I wondered if you might talk to her.'

'Me?' Anna shook her head in confusion. 'Why would Carmen talk to me?'

'*I* do,' he responded simply. 'Look, Carmen is going to hit the salons and the shops when she gets here. I thought I might tell her that you are scaring the locals and need a decent wardrobe.'

'That's a horrible thing to say.'

'I say a lot of horrible things,' he said, smiling. 'I don't always mean them, though. This way, Carmen will think there's a reason for you to go with her.'

'Why are you doing this?'

'Because I want you to talk to Carmen and maybe tell me what's going on.'

'I'm not going to break her confidence—to spy and then report back to you.'

'You're not a doctor or a priest! You don't need to take her secrets to the grave,' he said. 'Just let me know if she's okay. Because I swear there is something going on in her head, and I'm worried. Will you *try* speaking with her for me, please?'

'I'll try...'

'Okay.' He stood. 'I should go.'

'Yes.'

She saw him to the door and something close to panic quietly hit her—because she found she didn't know how to say goodbye.

It was bad enough with him here, but without him...

'*Hasta luego...*'

He left without a backward glance.

CHAPTER TEN

SEBASTIÁN FIXED HIS eyes on the road and tried not to notice the blue, blue Mediterranean or the glistening white yachts. And when he opened his window he quickly closed it again, because he did not want the scent of summer clouding his brain.

'Why are you doing this?' she had asked him.

Because he wanted to spoil her. Because she deserved to be spoiled.

To prevent himself thinking of Anna, he called his sister.

'I don't want to spend a day with Anna,' she sighed. 'She's boring.'

'Carmen…' He held in a tense breath. 'Just sort things out. Get the things she likes wrapped and sent to the villa without her knowing.' He gave her the address. 'Maybe go to a salon. I don't know…'

He tried to be himself, as he usually would be— curt, rude, nothing his problem. But the old him would not have given a damn that Emily's friend was feeling awkward in her clothes…

'Listen,' he said to his sister. 'I don't want Alejandro and Emily worrying about her. They have enough going on right now.'

'Okay.'

'So be nice and… I don't know…involve alcohol or something…'

He ended the call, annoyed at Carmen. He

thought of Anna, feeling awkward in the boutiques and salons with his difficult sister. *He* should be the one doing this…

But she'd upped the demands, his cynical mind reminded him. A holiday!

She had looked him in the eye and asked for more.

And he had said no.

Jerez was a couple of hours away, and when he arrived there was a serious amount of work waiting, given neither he nor Alejandro had been in for the past two days.

Good—he could immerse himself in that, he thought.

Only he found himself staring out of the window as his PA filled him in on everything she'd rescheduled.

And then Alejandro's PA came in and told him of the commitments in his brother's diary…

'The next three months?' she checked. 'Or will he be back sooner?'

'I don't know,' Sebastián said honestly.

He took a breath and looked out of the window. The blue sky seemed so vivid, he thought.

Somehow he got through a meeting, then another, and another, but finally he went up to the rooftop terrace. His engagement photos had been taken there. They'd toasted the gorgeous sunset with their own sherry, of course, for the camera's sake, but he'd frowned when Ella had taken a sip.

'You're having a baby,' he'd reminded her, in his usual blunt way.

He'd stood up here, getting those photos done, feeling impatient to get back to work.

Now, when there was work to be done, he was impatient to follow that blue sky all the way back to Puerto Banús.

He could not take a holiday now—and it wasn't just the impossible timing of it.

She wanted more from him. And although Sebastián was used to that, the conflict he felt now was because he found himself wanting to give more, despite his brain telling him not to...found himself talking to her more and revealing things he never shared with anybody.

And now here he sat, watching the sun starting to dip, wanting more.

Six nights...

They were already down to five now—four if he left it until tomorrow. Then there was the family party he was planning for Saturday, so that took it down to three. He liked the safety of that low number, the expiry date written in permanent ink...

Carmen messaged, conceding:

She's actually nice. We had a great day.

He didn't respond, because usually he wouldn't care that Emily's friend had had a great day.

Yet he did.

He did care.

Then the phone went again, and it was Anna.

He let it go to voicemail, then dialled the number to listen to her message, but she hadn't left one.

'Sebastián?'

His PA came onto the terrace, no doubt wondering what time she might get home. Spanish work days were long ones, but it was nearing ten o'clock…

'Go home.' Sebastián gave her a thin smile. 'Oh, and one more thing.'

She turned around. 'Tomorrow you're going to have to rework the schedule.'

'I already have.'

'I mean, again.'

'Oh.'

'I'm taking the rest of the week off.'

He really did have a brilliant PA. Because, to her credit, she didn't blink. He just saw her jaw tighten and then she pushed out a smile.

'Of course. I'll tell people it is a family emergency.'

'No,' Sebastián said. 'Just say that I am on vacation.'

The drive felt far shorter tonight than it had this morning—as if the road itself was hurrying him back to be with her. He just seemed to slice his way through time and space until he stepped out of the vehicle and heard the throb of music in the air and the palm leaves rustling overhead.

He knew he had made the right decision.

'Hola,' he said as she opened the door wearing a robe, with her hair lighter than when he had left her that morning. The redness in her skin had calmed down too—or was it that she had make-up on?

'Sebastián!' Anna was startled. 'I thought you were back in Jerez.'

'Briefly,' he said. 'You look hot.'

'No, the air-conditioning is on…' She paused. 'Oh, you mean…' She swallowed at his directness. 'Thank you. We got our hair and make-up done.'

'Can I come in?'

She was about to pull open the door, but then remembered her sewing was out in the lounge.

'Actually…' She cringed again. 'Can you just…?'

'Wait?'

'Yes.'

'While you tidy up?' he smiled.

'Yes.'

Quickly she moved her sewing project into her case, and before she headed back to the door to let him in Anna allowed herself a moment to take a deep breath and exhale slowly to calm her racing heart.

She had been sitting alone in her villa, doing her sewing, verging on crying. Dressed in new clothes—a silver dress and gorgeous underwear—she'd felt like Cinderella without a ball to go to, and she had taken off the dress and hurled it at the floor.

She was in the sexiest port in the world, dressed up to the nines, and she was…sewing!

And then the sexiest man in the world had shown up at her door.

Slow down, she told her beating heart—because he was clearly here to find out about Carmen, and actually she did have something to tell him.

'Come through,' she said, trying to breathe through her mouth and avoid the rich scent of the air whenever he was near. 'Carmen and I had a great day, and I came back to find this.' She pointed to several designer bags in her bedroom.

'A bed?'

'No!'

'I can only see the bed,' he said, and she tensed. Because he was so potent that the bags seemed to have faded and the bed was all she could see too.

'You spent far too much. You didn't need to do that.'

'So?' He shrugged and took a seat on the same chair she had been on.

'That's my seat,' Anna said.

'Come and sit here with me, then.'

He seemed lighter somehow. She didn't know this Sebastián—this lighter, less intense version of him.

She tried to get back to the reason he was here… took a seat on the sofa. 'We went shopping, and got our hair done, and—'

He closed his eyes, as if in frustration, and at

her halting words took a breath and nodded for her to go on.

'She's okay,' Anna said, not wanting to break Carmen's confidence, and yet wanting to let Sebastián know it wasn't that anything dark had taken place with her ex. 'She didn't want to talk at first. I mean, she doesn't know me… But when we were getting our hair done I told her how I haven't been on a date in years…'

'To get her to talk?'

'Yes,' Anna said.

'You didn't have to exaggerate that much.'

He smiled his gorgeous, arrogant smile and Anna opened her mouth to correct him. He didn't seem to quite get it that she'd told Carmen a painful truth in an attempt to get her to open up.

It was immaterial, Anna decided, choosing not to labour the point.

'We spoke a lot. I told Carmen about some of the nastier things Willow's father said when we broke up.'

'Okay…' The smile was wiped off his face and he was serious now. 'What *did* he say to you?'

'We're talking about Carmen.' Anna put up her hand, because she was not about to get into a discussion of her ex. 'You're right—what happened with her ex was nasty, but she's okay. It's only her feelings that are hurt…'

'Okay…'

Sebastián looked both frustrated and concentrating hard. He was clearly concerned about his sister, but that didn't seem to be the whole reason he was here.

'I think she's moving on from it.'

'Thank you.' He nodded. 'I'm glad that she's spoken to someone.' He hesitated. 'To you.'

'It's not just…' Anna paused.

There was one other thing Anna wanted to share about her meeting with Carmen, because she honestly didn't know if she'd handled it right.

'It's not just about the break-up. I do think she's working through that…'

'What then?' He frowned. 'Maria?'

'Not just that either.' Anna worried at her lip for a moment. 'I don't know if I should say anything…'

'Anna, whatever your opinion of me, surely you can accept that I have my sister's best interests at heart?'

'I know you do. It's just that she said something, and I'm honestly not sure if my response was the correct one.'

'What was it about?'

'Riding,' Anna said. 'Her career.'

'Okay…'

'We went for dinner and she asked about my family. I usually don't say very much but, like I said, I was trying to get her to open up, so I told her that I'd fallen out with my parents over Willow.'

He was really concentrating, Anna could see.

'I think she's worried that your father would be

disappointed if…' She saw that his frown remained. .
'If she changed paths or took a break.'

He stared back at her.

'She was going to tell him that she wanted to
give it up a few months ago, but he got ill and she
didn't know how to.'

'She wants to stop riding?'

'I think so. I told her she was worrying need-
lessly. I said that it was clear to me that her father loved her, whatever she did.' She swallowed.
'I hope I said the right thing?'

'Of course.'

He nodded, but there was something in his voice
that told her she might have steered Carmen wrong.

'I mean, I was just trying to—'

'It's fine,' he reassured her. 'It's good that she's
spoken to you.'

She nodded, still unsure if she'd messed up. 'I
tried to call you and tell you. You didn't have to
drive back.'

'I didn't drive back because of Carmen,' he said.

'Then why?'

'Because…'

She was used to him ruthlessly shutting down
any topic he did not wish to discuss, so she accepted that was all she was going to get. But he
changed all that with the addition of two words.

'Because you're here.'

There was something missing, surely? Her brain
kept trying to join the dots…

'Because you're here...'

'I took some time off,' Sebastián told her. 'I am on vacation.'

'Because of the baby?'

'No, because of what you said about wanting more than a one-night stand.' He gave her a slow smile. 'You will get your holiday...'

Looking at him really was like staring into the sun, Anna thought, because he was simply dazzling. So much so that she had to look away.

All her wishes had suddenly come true, yet she was afraid.

Anna looked at the bags scattered on the bed and heard her demand for a holiday with him in a less savoury way now.

'Do we have crossed wires?' she asked.

'Meaning?'

'I want time with you,' Anna said. 'Not...'

'I'm not hiring you, Anna.' He laughed. 'I want you to love it here,' he said. 'I want you to have the holiday you deserve.'

'Why?' she croaked.

'I like you,' he said, and only now did he falter slightly. 'I'd like a holiday with you. But as long as we're clear: no future. No falling in love. No—'

'What if...?' she cut in, but then halted, because she had a dreadful feeling it might be way too late for that.

No! She was not ruining this by getting overly emotional. Back in the real world she would see that this was not, nor ever could be, love. So she obliterated that thought from her mind.

'You were saying…?' he checked, because she knew he never missed a beat. 'What if…?'

Anna knew she had to fill the gap. Usually she would be embarrassed to bring it up, but now was grateful for the reason to blame her blush.

'What if I told you I'd gone on the Pill?'

'Oh? But, no…' He shook his head. 'We're not getting *that* close. I will take care of those details.'

He was so absolute with his boundaries that she couldn't help but ask, 'Why don't you let anyone get close to you?'

'I don't want to answer that.'

Anna was bold. Sure, she had her hang-ups, and was shy in certain things, but she dug deep and found that boldness so she could stare back at him, quietly demanding a different response.

Finally he gave one. 'I'm as incapable of love as the woman who birthed me.'

'No.'

'Anna, *yes*.' He was absolute. 'I'm not going to say the acceptable thing just because it's what you want to hear. I don't want love.' He offered another truth. 'I *do* want some time with you, though…'

'You are here until Sunday?' she checked, because if he left in the morning she would never forgive herself—let alone him.

'I have packed my bucket and spade.'

'Stop it!' She laughed, but her breathing was shallow and fast.

'I'm going to give you the holiday of your life.'

Never had she thought he'd agree to it. This was going to be a holiday—a real holiday—her first since she couldn't remember when. A holiday with the most stunning man ever to have come into her line of vision.

'No tears at the end,' he warned. 'Because it ends on Sunday morning. No exceptions.'

Perhaps… But Anna knew that she would possibly live off the memories for ever.

He crooked his finger and she stood and walked over to him, a little unsure if she was up to this, and still wondering if she was somehow dreaming…

He pulled her down onto his lap.

'Not just sex,' she said, as he unknotted the belt of her robe. 'Because when I said I wanted a holiday—'

'Anna,' he cut in, 'leave the details to me.'

'No,' Anna said, playing with the heavy silk of his loosened tie. 'I want a piece of that black heart.'

'You don't,' he said.

'Just a sliver,' Anna said, and kissed his very plump mouth.

She didn't know quite why, but she felt more resolute when she was with him. She kissed his scratchy cheek and then his temple…

'Let me look at you,' he said.

He pulled apart her robe and looked at her gorgeous new underwear. More than looked. He ran a finger over the lacy fabric and then moved his hand over the curve of her breast. It was the slowest perusal…unbearable in its exquisiteness.

He slid the sleeves of the robe down her arms and lifted her so that he could toss the robe to the floor. He turned her so she sat facing him, her thighs now astride his, and all he did was look. She felt as if her skin might blister and her lips might part and beg for him.

'What *are* you up to?' he asked.

'Up to?'

'What is it you have to hide when I come to the door?'

She blushed because he knew she was hiding something. 'I'm not going to tell you.'

'Tell me…' he said, running a warm finger over the lace that covered a very private place and then slipping it beneath the fabric.

'Oh…' She was lifting onto her knees at the touch of his skilled fingers. 'Don't tear them…' she said, because she liked her new knickers.

'Take them off,' he said, and removed his hand. 'And go and get it.'

'What?'

'Whatever you're using,' he said in a low whisper, his voice gruff in her ear. 'I can use it on you…'

She pulled back and stared at him. 'I genuinely don't know what you mean.'

'Don't be embarrassed,' he said. 'You don't have to hide your toys.'

'You think I'm in here with a sex toy!' She was shocked, and embarrassed for a moment, but because she was in his arms she found she had started laughing. 'You don't know me at *all*!'

'Every time I come to the door you're half-dressed and you make me wait.'

'Please don't ask me, but I promise you I am really not having the kind of fun you think.' She playfully punched his suited arm, and knew she was blushing even as she met his eyes.

And for Sebastián things suddenly changed again.

'You don't know me at all...' she had said, and yet he wanted to.

There was an innocence to her green eyes, an honesty in her gaze that he was struggling to recognise—because usually he trusted no one.

Since the wedding he had not been able to completely erase her from his mind. Not even in his usual way.

The wild parties aboard his yacht had ended along with his engagement, but in recent months there had been no guests aboard his yacht at all. Since meeting Anna he had simply been unable to indulge in his once favourite escape.

It was just sex, he told himself as she met his gaze.

He pulled her higher up onto his lap, yet could not

stop staring at her eyes, exploring them, as he might gaze into a seemingly still lake and know there was a whole world beneath that glassy surface.

It was more than sex—whatever he might tell himself.

Just for a little while he wanted to know again the pleasure of her conversation, her company—and, yes, to get to know her better. He wanted her to laugh, to smile, to have the fun she deserved, and he actually ached to be the one to give that to her.

To give her a small piece of his black heart...

A sliver...

'Get dressed,' he said.

Anna blinked, because she'd also been trapped in his gaze, feeling hot in his arms, and getting naked was the only thing on her mind.

'Dressed?'

'We're going out.'

'Sebastián!'

She was both bemused and smiling as he shifted her closer to the press of his erection and left her in no doubt that he was as turned on as she. She moved in to kiss him, but he turned so her lips met his cheek.

'I can't go out like this.'

'Oh, but you can,' he told her. 'I'm going to date you, Anna Douglas.'

CHAPTER ELEVEN

AWKWARD IN A shiny silver dress that was so not her, Anna walked with Sebastián towards the port.

'You look incredible,' he told her. 'Stop pulling at it.'

'There is nowhere else I'd wear this,' she admitted. 'I only tried it on to make Carmen laugh.'

She reached for his hand because…well, because she wanted to.

'I don't hold hands,' he said.

'When you buy six-inch heels for a woman,' Anna said, 'you have a duty to hold her hand if you don't want her to fall.'

'I'll catch you if you do.'

Anna laughed, feeling on a dizzy high as she hobbled along the jetty.

Perhaps it was because she was so dreadful in heels that he finally relented and took her hand.

If the shoe fits, the foot is forgotten…

Anna thought of the saying again, because with his hand around hers she forgot about the heels and the tight silver dress that was so inappropriate her mother would faint if she saw her in it.

'Where are we going?' she asked. 'To a bar? A club?'

'To my favourite place.'

She felt a flutter of excitement as they walked along the jetty. Anna knew nothing about yachts, but she knew beauty when she saw it. She glimpsed, too, that welcome feeling that he had told her about. For this was no luxury villa or hotel. It was his home.

'Bienvenido a bordo, Sebastián!' He was greeted by an immaculate man in dark trousers and a white shirt. 'Welcome aboard, *señorita*. I am Capitán Dante.' He was friendly, yet formal and respectful. 'May I ask that you remove your shoes?'

'For my decking,' Sebastián explained, and then saw her reach unsteadily to lean on the cabin wall. 'Let me help.'

'Oh…'

And then he was kneeling down and removing her shoes.

She swallowed at the touch of his hands as he undid the tiny buckles. 'Do Russian supermodels have to take their heels off?'

He let out a short burst of laughter.

Removing the silver heels, he placed them in a basket, and all she could wonder was how she might feel when she strapped them on again, because there was so much to take in.

They went up some stairs and came out on a deck so polished and soft beneath her feet that it felt like carpet. The furnishings were expensive and gorgeous—huge pale grey sofas, with tasteful splashes of colour to bring them alive—and a waiter stood at the bar, where Sebastián ordered cocktails.

'Romero's own,' he said.

It was sherry and bitter orange and something else, but she was almost too giddy to take it in as the yacht manoeuvred out of the marina.

'Have you eaten?' Sebastián asked.

'I have.'

He spoke in Spanish and soon little nibbles were being placed on a low candlelit table. She admired the glass tumblers that held tealights. They were engraved with stars to match those shining overhead. The night sky was divine, and she felt as if the stars might have been individually placed there just for her.

'Dance?' Sebastián said, once they had anchored away from the prying eyes of the marina, and he offered his hand.

The smooth deck was their dance floor, but the real luxury was being held in his arms.

'I adore your back,' he said as he held her close and ran a finger down her naked spine. 'I mean,' he said, 'you really have a beautiful back.'

They danced—and not the way they had at the wedding.

He kissed her shoulder and then grazed it with his teeth. He pulled her tighter in to him and kissed her neck. If he wasn't holding her she would be on her knees, she thought.

'The crew…'

'Shh…' he said. 'They're below.'

It felt as if they were alone in the world...alone under the stars. The slight motion of the yacht on the waves, the breeze on her skin and the heat of his mouth entranced her as he held her and kissed her neck, as if the tender skin he was focussed upon was the most vital spot on planet earth.

He took her right to the edge, and she almost folded in his arms. Then he removed his mouth, his hand, his hard body. It was disorientating to be giddy with lust and then led down some steps that were softer even than the deck.

'The floor...what is it?'

Every sensation was new.

'Leather,' he said, and guided her into the master cabin.

This was his home. That was her one coherent thought as she stepped inside. There was Spanish art on the walls, and she glimpsed an oil painting of ancient Jerez, almost out of place in such modern surroundings.

Yet not out of place, Anna thought as he slowly stripped her naked while devouring her with his mouth. It was as contradictory as this man.

Finally he kissed her all over, as he had promised that night at the wedding.

And each stroke of his tongue and velvet kiss was an apology for not ending that morning as he should have.

He undressed himself between hot, decadent kisses. She was rendered unable to assist, because each suck on her pale breasts had her bunching the crisp sheet beneath her and gasping for breath.

Sebastián was lost as he watched her breasts fall to the side a little—as real breasts did, not silicone mounds. Her stomach was flat, yet soft too. And her intimate curls were like kisses to his face as he moved down and parted her thighs.

'I want to see you,' he said as he rolled on a condom.

Anna watched as he looked, and the desire in his eyes had her clenching in anticipation and then sobbing as his mouth came down to kiss her where no mouth ever had before.

His jaw was rough, his tongue probing, and she raised herself up on her elbows briefly, to watch how absorbed he was in his task, then gave in and lay back.

She moved one hand down and gripped his hair, not sure if she was pulling him back because the contact was too intense to bear, or pressing him closer because she needed more.

He made love to her with his mouth and did not relent even when she came. He tasted her passion fully, and when she was spent, one leg draped over his shoulder, he knelt up.

'You taste incredible…'

She was panting as he looked down at her, and then he kissed her with lips that were shiny from *her*. They rolled to face each other, tumbling, still kissing, until he was on his back and she was astride him.

It felt different from when they'd been in that chair at the villa. Not just because of their lack of clothes, or the bed. It was more that they had changed since then.

Then, it had been sex.

Now, it was…

Anna didn't quite know how to describe the comparison—just that when she lowered herself down onto him there was synergy between them, both wanting more from the other.

She had never been on top before, but did not feel uncertain—just inexperienced. She closed her eyes as he filled her, because the deep penetration felt so new.

'Come here,' he demanded roughly, and pulled her head down towards him.

Her hands moved behind his shoulders and they kissed as he bucked and she responded until she found a rhythm she liked.

Awkwardly, for his shoulders and his body were big, she moved her hands to his chest. But soon there was no awkwardness in Anna, just a sense of urgency. His hands were on her breasts, thorough in their movements, and she felt the solid wall of his chest beneath her hands.

'So good…' he said, and then he said something

in Spanish, and reached for a pillow to put it behind his head, so he could see her better.

Her buttocks were sliding on his thighs and his hands came up to her hips. But then he removed them.

'Help me,' Anna said, because she wanted his hands exactly where they had been...she wanted the grip and guidance of them.

'You!' he said, thrusting as she ground down.

He was denying his hands what they wanted as a form of self-torture. For now he wanted to watch her face change as she sought deeper pleasure from him. He played with her hair, pinched her nipple—anything that would help him fight not to finish until she was ready.

'Oh...'

Anna closed her eyes in deep concentration as he stroked her, every part of her body feeling spent already. Her thighs ached and she was holding back a sob of frustration—or perhaps a scream.

But then his hands slid down her damp, flushed body and took her hips firmly. She had never been so loose and so tense at the same time, because now he grasped her and moved within her at a pace she would never have found on her own.

She heard herself making humming sounds, unintelligible sounds, but they only made his grip on her hips tighter.

And then he stilled her, and Anna felt a final powerful swell within her and choked out a sound as he released himself into her.

The low shout that accompanied it was so intense that it pulled at her centre…pulled so tightly that she gave up moving, just closed her eyes and enjoyed the intimate beats of her own body's release and the fading pulse of him within her.

'I drove back for that,' he said as they lay side by side.

She gave a soft laugh. 'You can go now, then.' Anna sat up and reached for the iced water that had thoughtfully been left by the bedside. 'Oh, wait… I forgot. It's your yacht…'

It was a tease, not a threat—just light joking after something both knew had been incredible.

'Watch this,' he said. 'Lie on your back.'

Anna did so, and he lay beside her and pressed a button on a remote control.

The ceiling parted and they were bathed in stars.

'I kept it closed in case there was a drone.'

She'd fallen asleep in his arms the night of the wedding, but this time Anna was in no doubt that what they had experienced together had been beautiful—that the yacht, the stars, the pleasure had all been incredible.

What she did not know was that in that moment she'd been gifted a sliver of his heart…

CHAPTER TWELVE

'WHAT TIME IS IT?'

She woke to piercing sunlight and there was Sebastián, pulling back the drapes to reveal the dazzling ocean.

'Midday,' he said.

'Oh, my G—' She stopped, because she didn't ever blaspheme.

'Oh, my God?' he said for her, and he laughed.

'What's so funny?'

'All the things you don't do or say. We didn't go to sleep until dawn.'

'True.'

'Breakfast is ready.'

'You mean lunch?'

'No, you're on Spanish time,' he said as she climbed out of bed and picked up her once lovely but now crumpled silver dress.

He frowned. 'Why would you wear that?'

'Because it's all I have with me.' She laughed. 'Gosh, I didn't take very good care of it, did I?'

'Blame me,' Sebastián said. 'Go and shower,' he said. 'Your dress will be taken care of, and I'll find a shirt or something for you.'

She felt very untogether as she came out of the shower to…yes, a shirt. Her dress and underwear had been whisked away… And so, wearing just the shirt, carefully pulling it down over her bottom, she climbed the stairs and said good morning to the smiling Capitán Dante, who was having coffee with Sebastián, and stood as she ventured on deck.

'Buenos días,' he said, and Anna smiled, while wanting to curl up and hide.

'I feel…' She knew she was cringing as she took a seat and then halted as coffee was poured.

'Gracias,' Sebastián said, and told the server he would take it from here. 'What's wrong?'

'They all know I stayed the night.'

'Yes.'

'And they've got my underwear!' She shot him a look. 'At least at the hotel and villa it was a bit more anonymous.' She broke apart a pastry. 'The sun is so bright…' She caught herself. 'I sound like that awful woman from the hotel.'

'Believe me, you don't,' he said.

They ended up on loungers, and he kept looking over to her, as she constantly checked that she was covered.

'You could take that off and they wouldn't care.'

'I'd care,' Anna said. 'I'm sure they've seen plenty, but they won't be seeing me.'

Even so, as they lay together quietly in the sun, she felt the tension leave her. She lay with her eyes closed, listening to the lap of the water and the caw of gulls, and then she heard Sebastián talking to someone.

'Here,' he said, and she opened her eyes.

He blocked out the sun and for a second she

thought her eyes must still be closed and she was dreaming. But, no, he handed her a small pink bag with silky rope handles.

'What's this?'

She opened it and took out a very small gold bikini. She blinked at this Aladdin's Cave world, where thoughts and wishes came true.

'Thank you.' She was touched that he'd noted her discomfort. 'I'll go and put it on.'

'There's no need.'

He handed her the bikini bottoms and she pulled them on beneath the shirt, and then he handed her the top and she tied up the neck while still wearing his shirt.

He rolled his eyes as she held it over her front and he tied the back. 'Better?' he asked.

'Yes.' She looked up at him. 'I called Emily and I said I'd visit her this evening. She's moving into a suite on the NICU.'

He nodded with his eyes closed and she guessed he'd already done his due diligence with his brother.

'How's your daughter?'

'She's having fun with her grandparents.' Anna smiled, but didn't elaborate, sure he was just being polite.

But then he asked a question. 'Have you told her about the new baby?'

'Not yet.'

How odd, Anna thought, to be lying in a tiny gold bikini and having such a normal conversation.

So normal that as she answered him she rolled onto her front to look at him as she spoke.

'I've told my mother, but I want to wait till I'm home to explain it to Willow. I think she'll be upset.'

'Because the baby is so small?'

'Because she isn't here to see her. I think it would just overwhelm her.'

Sebastián nodded and from behind his dark glasses stared up at the sky. There was not a single cloud in sight. He could recall lying on a beach in Corsica, with Ella beside him, a sparkling ring on her finger, and feeling no peace in his soul…

'Does her father help?'

He'd asked Anna about him before and she'd closed that down, but he wanted to be more personal now.

'No.'

'Does he see her?' he asked, and looked from the sky to her green eyes as he removed his shades.

'No.'

'Is Willow really why you fell out with your parents?'

She nodded. 'They think it was just a one-night stand.'

'Even I could tell them that it wouldn't have been.'

She blinked in surprise. 'Are you forgetting our one night?'

'Never!' He smiled and looked at her. 'I'm very good at seduction.'

'I had noticed.'

'I had to use all my skills—and they are considerable—to get you into bed… Anyway, we didn't sleep together the night we met, even though we were flirting on sight.'

'No!'

'Yes,' he refuted. 'I wanted you the first second I saw you.'

He knew he was spinning her mind, because while she thought back to the day they'd met he got back to the conversation they'd been having before.

'So, you and Willow's father weren't a one-night stand?'

'No.'

She had only ever told Emily the truth, and even then it had been a crisp version, leaving out all the feelings.

She tried to do the same now. 'He was a visiting professor when I was at university.'

'Tut-tut,' he said. 'He should have known better.'

'I *was* twenty-one.'

'He should still have known better!' he said.

And she stared back and knew then that there would be no 'crisp' versions when she was with Sebastián. His black eyes gave her permission to speak, to search herself, to be honest with herself.

'I was so naïve… I thought he was…' She frowned, because how she'd felt then was so pale in comparison to what she was experiencing now. 'I thought he was fascinating. But I was just…'

'What?'

'I'd never had a boyfriend before.'

'He was hardly a boy,' he sneered.

She knew his displeasure was not aimed at her, and she knew something else too: that he was on her side in this conversation. It was an unfamiliar feeling, after so many arguments and accusations, to know that she didn't have to speak defensively.

She didn't quite know how to tell him the full story, though.

'He was so angry when he found out I was pregnant…' She shook her head, not wanting to go on.

'How angry?'

'Just shouting…'

Anna opened her mouth to speak and then closed it, then opened it again. He watched her silently floundering and knew how hard it was for her to confide in him.

He could also guess what might be eating her up.

Maybe if he told her his truth, then she might open up? Anna had done it for Carmen—had given a piece of herself in order to learn more.

'Anna, did he use protection?'

'No.'

'So what right did he have to be angry? I've never wanted children, and I'm always careful, but even when Ella told me she was pregnant I never got angry.'

'Were you upset?'

'Maybe inwardly,' he admitted. 'But I didn't show it. I figured she was already upset enough.'

'But were *you*?'

'I'm very careful not to have unprotected sex, but when she showed me the ultrasound image I wasn't angry or shouting. Babies happen. You deal with it.'

Anna found she was holding her breath—perhaps because she was recalling Willow's father's reaction.

'I didn't love her, but I wanted to be a better parent than mine had been.' he said, as if trying to explain his thought-process. 'I didn't want to be absent, like Maria, even though I know I can be cold and selfish like her.'

'No.' Anna shook her head, adamant, for she knew he was involved with his family, there for his family.

'Yes,' he said. 'I like my career, my own space, and I would never commit myself to another person. But then I found out I was to be a father...'

'So you proposed?'

'Looking back, it was perhaps a knee-jerk reaction.' He shrugged. 'It would never have worked. And then...' He glanced over. 'I'm sure you've read what happened.'

'I want to hear what happened from you,' Anna said.

'We had an argument,' he told her. 'Here on the yacht. She was drinking—not in front of me, but Dante let me know that more champagne had been ordered.'

'I'm not with you...'

'He let me know in his very discreet way that my supplies were being topped up.'

'I'd better not crack open the bar, then.'

'Of course you can,' he said lightly, but then he looked serious. 'I dared to suggest to Ella that it might not be good for the baby. I asked to accompany her to her next doctor's appointment, and it was shortly after that when she told me she'd lost the baby.' He looked at her. 'Anna, there never was a baby.'

'But you said you saw the ultrasound picture.'

'You can buy them online, apparently.'

'She was lying all along?'

'Ella is too arrogant in her attitude towards staff to comprehend that I talk with my crew and they with me. She was in the spa, laughing with her friend about how I'd believed her. My crew don't spy. They don't judge. But...'

'They were looking out for you?'

'Yes.'

'Well!' She didn't know what to say. 'Why did you let her get away with it?'

'I told her what I thought, believe me.'

'I mean, with everyone else?'

'It's none of their business. I don't care what's said about me. *I* know the truth and so does she...'

'I'd be screaming it from the rooftops.'

'No.' He looked at her. 'It's hard to reveal what really hurts.'

He reached over and pushed her hair back from her face. He was not smoothing his way to a kiss, just trying to be gentle as he asked a question he was rather certain he already knew the answer to.

'Did you know he was married?'

'Of course not!' She was alarmed. 'How did you know…?'

'Why else would you keep his secret?'

He watched as she started to cry. He still had no handkerchief to offer, but he handed her the shirt she'd discarded instead.

'I had no idea…'

She felt stunned that he had guessed, and yet she felt as if he knew her—that he had taken care to work her out before diving in with his summing up.

'He said it would end his career, his marriage…'

'Poor professor,' he said, and then uttered a word that even in her fragile state had her pursing her lips.

'Don't say that.'

'I save it for particular types,' he said, 'and he is one.'

'Yes.' She wiped her nose on his exquisite shirt and thought of his laundry service. 'Sorry…'

'Go ahead.'

'He gave me money to have an abortion…told me to "take care of it".'

'He knows you kept the baby?'

'Yes, but he doesn't want anything to do with her.'

'Does he help financially?'

'No. I could have insisted, but I didn't want to break up his family.'

'Why can't you tell your parents the truth?'

'I'm ashamed.'

'You shouldn't be.'

'But I am,' Anna admitted, and then she told him her biggest fear. 'I don't know what to tell Willow. I just tell her our relationship didn't work out, but she's starting to ask more and more about him. How do I tell her that he has another family and wants nothing to do with her?'

She liked it that he listened carefully and thought for a long while before answering—even if she was sure there was nothing he could say that she hadn't thought of already.

'Get rid of that shame before you tell her.'

Anna looked up, because that actually sounded like a plan. 'Yes…' She blew out a breath. 'And I'll tell her in stages, I guess.'

'Yes.'

'Do you know…?' She looked out at the ocean, at the glorious day, and let herself think of the topic she'd fought so hard to avoid. 'I just wish he'd ended things nicely.'

Sebastián found that he'd tensed, because he'd been ruthless at ending things too many times. He had cut people out if they dared to get too close.

'Even if he didn't want to be part of our future, I hate that it ended in a row.' Anna gave herself a little shake and then concluded again. 'I just wish it had ended nicely.'

She took a breath of salty sea air, as if she felt better for telling him.

'I'm sorry for what happened to you,' she told him.

'We live and learn,' he said, but then he halted, because it felt for a moment as though he'd learnt the wrong lesson from his brief engagement.

He'd learnt not to trust.

CHAPTER THIRTEEN

'HEY, YOU.'

Sebastián smiled as Anna came up on deck, her hair rumpled and her eyes blinking from sleep. He returned reluctantly to his online conversation as she poured coffee.

Anna wore one of his T-shirts, although someone on the crew had collected her things from the villa and they now hung in his immaculate wardrobe alongside the silver dress.

'Do you want breakfast now?' he offered. 'Or I should only be another hour.'

Are you online...? she mouthed, indicating the screen.

He was so at ease with himself that he frowned, trying to understand what she was asking, but then he reminded himself this was Anna.

He stepped out of the online meeting.

'Anna, I was just asking if you wanted breakfast.'

He did not understand how the smile he had greeted her with as she'd surfaced on deck, the look in his eyes and his subsequent reaction, had told all present at the meeting—including Alejandro—that his latest temporary lover had appeared.

'I don't want anyone to know, remember?' she told him.

It was the one part of their agreement they hadn't properly thrashed out.

He still could not understand what the issue was. Her insistence on secrecy had begun to irritate him, in fact. But for Anna clearly the issue was huge.

And so he kissed her worry away, smothering her in kisses once the meeting had ended.

It was forgotten—or rather, lost—in a whirl of jet-skis, water bikes and even a slide put out by the crew that went from the yacht straight into the ocean.

'Why have you got an inflatable slide?' she asked.

'Because…' he said, and then gave her a slow, wicked smile. 'Have you never wondered about those emergency slides on a plane?'

'We're not on a plane.'

'Evacuate!' he exclaimed urgently, and stalked towards her menacingly.

'What!'

'Do not stop to collect your personal belongings…'

His deep voice was urgent, and she felt goosebumps—not so much at the imagined scenario, but because Sebastián was having fun. Real fun. And so was she. The type of fun where she screamed and laughed at the same time as he picked her up.

'Don't!' she shrilled, as he carried her to the edge.

The edge of the yacht, the edge of sheer joy, the edge of fear and ecstasy.

And she screamed as she bumped down the slide and skimmed the water for a second before crashing in.

He followed straight behind her, catching her waist and pulling her up to the surface. She did not want to know how deep the water was beneath them, or what lurked at the bottom.

She was in it.

And, oh, gosh, even as she laughed there was a new terror as she wrapped her legs around his waist and they kissed.

Because she was so deeply in…so deeply into him.

Her legs were wrapped around him…the sun was beating on her shoulders, her scalp, intensifying her feelings. His eyes were so black as she stared into them, his lashes so spiky, and now her smile was fading…

'Sebastián?'

She didn't know how to contain all that she felt… how to accept this deliciousness only for it to end… how to be his now and yet also to know that their days were numbered…how to return back to normal when they hit their expiry date…nor how to hide the passion he tapped not just in others but in her…

Tell him! Her own voice sounded in her head as she stared back at him. *Tell him how you are feel-*

ing, right this moment...right now. Tell him that you might just be falling in...

'I think—'

He interrupted her. 'Do you want to go again?'

Sebastián was either oblivious to the turmoil in her eyes, or actively preventing her from saying words he did not want to hear.

It was the latter, Anna was sure.

Yes, the latter.

He did not want to hear any declarations outside of the bedroom. He did not want empty words that held no meaning... Nothing could come of them, so why spoil it with lies? He was stopping her from ruining a very nice thing.

'No...' She declined a second go on the slide. 'Once was enough for me.'

They swam back and she climbed up the ladder, her legs a little wobbly not so much from the thrill of the slide, but more from the words she'd been about to say to him. Unwanted words, it would seem.

'I ought to visit Emily.'

'Sure. I'll get Dante to organise the tender,' Sebastián said, but then changed his mind. 'Or we could return to port and give the crew time to do a service.'

It was protocol, apparently, to give the crew time to do their work undisturbed.

It was incredible to lie on the private deck off the main cabin as the yacht was skilfully reversed in and docked, and yet Anna's heart was still thumping as she realised how close she'd come to saying too much. To ruining their temporary arrangement...

As Sebastián went up to speak with Dante she showered and washed her hair, her tanned limbs looking unfamiliar as she washed the ocean salt from her body. Drying off, she looked at her gorgeous new clothes, but chose the familiar long skirt and cheesecloth top she had brought with her from home. She wondered if she was trying to find the old Anna...the sensible Anna who knew this could never last.

She called Willow, who seemed to have picked up a little Scottish accent!

'Three more sleeps, lassie,' Willow said.

'Yes, only three more sleeps,' Anna agreed— then inwardly panicked, because that meant only two nights left with Sebastián, because of the party on Saturday night.

How could it already be Thursday?

Their last night would likely be tomorrow...

It had gone by in a puff.

'I cannae see any photos of Emily, Mummy.'

'I'm sorry, darling.' Anna laughed at her daughter's quirky ways. 'I keep getting her to take photos of me. I'll sort that out now.'

'Can I talk to wee Emily?'

'Willow, stop!' Anna giggled. 'Emily's with Alejandro at the moment, but I'll get her to call you.'

Oh, Willow, Anna thought, sitting on the rumpled bed. She was desperate to see her daughter in person, and kept smiling long after the call had ended.

She wanted to tell Sebastián how Willow had just made her laugh, but she couldn't bear to be rewarded with only his polite, uncomprehending smile.

She came up on deck to discover that he was in another meeting. He excused himself from it and turned the microphone off when he saw her.

'I'm off,' Anna said. 'I might head back to the villa for a while.'

'Why don't you check out?'

'No…' Anna shook her head. And it wasn't because she had the blessed blanket to finish—it was more because she needed the bolthole, a place to escape to, in moments like this, when otherwise she might say too much.

She didn't say any of that, of course… 'Emily thinks I'm staying there.'

'Sebastián?' Capitán Dante came over. 'Carmen has come to visit.' He possibly saw Anna's reaction, because he dealt with it immediately. 'The first steward is talking to her.'

Sebastián, too, must have noticed her appalled expression, but he just shrugged. 'Carmen took you out for the day.' He shrugged. 'I'll tell her it was my turn.

'No!' She was adamant. 'I don't want her finding out. I'll go into the cabin.'

She heard his irritated sigh as she scuttled off.

The cabin was in the middle of being serviced, and she felt wretched for asking the crew to leave.

Another yacht protocol broken, Anna thought as she sat on the half-made bed.

Sebastián's sigh was born of irritation—and not only because Anna insisted that they hide what they were doing.

'You can't just drop in unannounced,' he scolded his demanding sister.

'Since when?' Carmen shrugged and threw herself dramatically onto a lounger.

'I mean it, Carmen. I could have had a lover here.'

'You always have lovers here.'

Not lately, Sebastián thought. *More specifically, not since the wedding.*

He'd been too pensive to party.

Then he said all that again in his mind and realised that he was thinking in English—as if explaining his thoughts to Anna—and he thought how that one might have made her smile.

Too pensive to party…

'Why are you smiling?' Carmen snapped. 'I just told you I'm dreading Saturday.'

'It's just a celebration for the baby.'

'For you, perhaps, but I'm flying back to Jerez with them,' Carmen said and then added. 'Maybe…'

He tried to focus because, thanks to Anna, he knew what was troubling his sister. 'What do you mean *maybe*?'

'I don't know if we'll still be talking. I've got something I want to tell Papá.'

He waited, but Carmen refused to elaborate, and he guessed it wasn't *his* approval she needed in order to give up riding.

'Carmen?'

'I don't want to discuss it with you. I want to talk to Papá. But Maria's always there. I hate it that he's let her move back in. I know I'm more than old enough to leave home—but it's not as simple as just moving out. What about the horses? And who's going to be there for Papá if she decides to leave again?'

'Carmen, you don't have to be his carer.'

His heart felt as if it were on a hoist, pulled in too many different directions.

And he understood all the angles: Anna hiding in his cabin, protecting her reputation from his, Carmen wanting to break free, feeling so utterly rejected by her mother and terrified her father might do the same, and as for Alejandro…

There was a notable absence of fear in him.

Sebastián felt the snap of one of the ropes as he realised he wasn't worried about Alejandro.

His brother had a baby in Intensive Care, and yet he knew he would be okay.

What kind of flawed logic was that?

Then he sat with the answer: Alejandro loved and was loved.

And Sebastián dared not love.

Not because of his brief and meaningless engagement, but because of his mother.

'Carmen…' He spoke gravely to his sister. 'You can talk to me. I do know—'

'You don't, though,' Carmen snapped. 'She didn't leave *you* when *you* were a baby.'

No, Maria had left for the final time when he was ten, and fifty times or more prior to that.

And he *did* know. Because when Maria de Luca smiled, she was dazzling. When she told you she was your *mamá*, and would always be there for you, it raised you high.

Then she discarded you, and you fell back down to earth.

Then she left his father crying, her babies fretful and bemused—especially if she'd fired the latest nanny before she left…

He knew well the poison on the tip of all her arrows.

And it terrified him to think he was like her— cold, career-focussed, unable to commit…

'Talk to me…' he said to his sister, but Carmen shook her head.

'I have to go and check in with Anna.'

'Why?'

'Alejandro asked me to take her out again.'

'Oh?'

'I think they feel guilty about how her holiday has turned out.'

'They have just had a premature baby.'

'Yes, but she doesn't get out much.' Carmen shrugged and accepted a drink from Dante, who knew her order well. 'She's barely been out since she had Willow.'

'What?' Sebastián tried to make light of it. 'She's a hermit?'

'No!' Carmen gave a half-laugh. 'But I don't think she has the time or money for a social life.' She took a sip of her drink. 'She hasn't been on a date since she had her daughter'

'Come off it!'

'No, she told me.'

'Maybe she meant she hasn't had a serious relationship,' Sebastián countered, but then he paused with his drink on its way to his mouth, because he knew Anna better than that.

Anna had told him herself that the wedding had been her first time away from her daughter, but he'd taken that as meaning her first trip overseas.

Had she meant her first *night* away?

Was he her first lover since Willow's father? Surely not…

'Anyway, she's getting back out there,' Carmen said. 'Getting her confidence back…'

Sebastián said nothing.

'And I'm going to do the same... Not that I'm looking to settle down,' Carmen added.

'Is Anna?' He knew he should feign uninterest, but he couldn't not ask.

'I think she wants a family—brothers and sisters for Willow.'

It took for ever for Carmen to leave, and even when she had, he sat on deck alone for several moments.

He didn't trust himself with Anna's blossoming heart.

Nor her with his.

Was Anna dipping her toes back in the water, reclaiming her confidence, *with him*?

She had to be—he had explicitly told her it was going nowhere and that he never wanted a partner or children. Let alone someone else's.

He was watching her change, right before his eyes, like a butterfly coming out of a chrysalis, and on Sunday morning that butterfly would fly away... Back to her family, who loved her, whether she believed it or not. Back to her daughter and her future plans...

The thought hurt more than it should.

But they were an impossible match and already getting too close.

No more.

He went down to Anna in the cabin...

'She's gone,' he said, then gave her a smile and

sat with her on the bed. 'I'm not usually berthed in the same port as my family. Mostly I sail away.'

'It's fine.' She looked up. 'I think it's nice that you're close to your family.'

'Carmen's about to stop by the villa and ask to take you out.'

Anna smiled at the irony. 'Is she okay?'

'Of course.'

'You look serious…'

'No.'

'I'm sorry for being pathetic,' Anna said. 'I just…'

'You don't want anyone finding out about us.'

'Not if we're not going anywhere.'

'Anna, you know we're not. You fly back on Sunday.'

'Yes, but—'

'I think,' Sebastián interrupted, 'we ought to let the crew in to service the cabin. And you need to visit Emily.'

'Sebastián—'

'Anna,' he cut in again. 'It's a holiday. It's not for ever.'

He would not let either of them forget that fact.

CHAPTER FOURTEEN

PUERTO BANÚS MIGHT be the perfect place for a holiday romance, but there was a wedge between them now and Anna couldn't quite put her finger on why.

They made love, they laughed… He gave her everything—except any further piece of that black heart.

There had been hospital visits, and trips back to the villa, but it wasn't the just the prospect of time with Sebastián that had her shaking as she trimmed the final thread of silk. It wasn't even the lure of the luxurious yacht that had her a little impatient as she carefully restitched the backing. It was the fact that their time was running out.

'I got to hold her!'

Emily was both smiling and crying when Anna took in the completed blanket.

'I actually feel like a mother now.'

'Of course you're a mother!' Anna hugged her friend.

'Alejandro is going to hold her tomorrow. It's too much for her to have us both all in one day,' Emily explained. 'How's Willow?'

'Wondering why there are so few photos of you,' Anna admitted.

'I'll put some make-up on and we can go outside and call her.'

'Thank you.'

Emily was brilliant with Willow, never letting

on about the drama in her heart, and Anna loved her friend so much for that.

'She's certainly enjoying Scotland,' Emily said as they stood outside for a moment longer, enjoying the breeze and the sun. And then she looked properly at her friend. 'You look different…'

'I've been lying in the sun,' Anna said.

'No, it's more than that…'

'I got my hair done.'

'I know—Carmen told me. You just look so…' Anna watched her friend as she struggled to place what was different.

Everything was different.

She had fallen for the very man Emily had warned her about. She'd been told it would hurt, and it did.

Maybe it was good that she was leaving on Sunday, Anna thought. Time was passing fast. And now this odd wall had gone up between them and she didn't know how to push through.

She and Emily told each other so much, but Anna did not want to share this. Emily knew her well, and would know she'd be hopeless at a casual relationship.

Emily would tell her what she knew already— that Sebastián was a playboy…that he went through women like most men went through socks…

And she didn't want future visits in Spain to be uncomfortable.

So she didn't tell her friend what was going on.

More than that, Anna was trying not to admit to herself what was going on in her heart.

Certainly she could not tell Sebastián.

She didn't want it to be Friday already, and yet it was.

They met at the marina, where they sat watching expensive cars and gorgeous people descending upon the hotspot.

'Are you looking forward to tomorrow?' Anna asked as she twirled the straw in her glass.

'It'll be like herding cats…'

Anna laughed and waited for him to elaborate.

He did not.

And so they finished their drinks and wandered the streets. She peered in designer shop windows at Fabergé eggs and all things incredible…

Sebastián looked at her face, lit up by the lights of the shop windows. He knew he'd let her get too close. But he also knew she was leaving and so he was pulling away…

It was best for both of them, he'd decided.

Tomorrow his family descended. Anna would be there—but not the Anna he had come to know.

She would be the Anna who denied they even existed.

They would ignore each other, or talk politely…

The way they would have to do now, whenever she returned see her friend.

'It will be nice.' She turned and looked at him. 'To have everyone see the baby. What time are they flying in?'

'We're meeting at the hotel at four,'

'The same one Carmen's staying at?'

'No.' He gave her the address. 'From there we'll head to the hospital. I've organised a private room. After that we'll head back to the yacht for a little celebration before they fly home.'

And the next day it would be Anna who would fly home.

End it now, his head said as they walked back to his yacht.

And he knew how to: as Anna spoke with Dante, Sebastián took out his phone and fired a quick text to his sister.

'Señorita Anna!' Dante greeted her. 'Welcome aboard.'

'*Gracias*, Capitán Dante.'

Anna smiled as she practised her Spanish, but as they chatted a thought occurred: would Dante greet her by name tomorrow?

Would Emily and his entire family find out that she had been spending time on the yacht? A lot of time actually!

'Carmen's dropping by,' Sebastián said.

'When?'

'After she's visited Emily.' He pocketed his phone as if it was Carmen who had messaged him. 'At least she gave me some notice this time.'

Anna had a wish—and it was a terrible wish. She wished his family would clear off. Or that she could stop the clock…that the world would just disappear and leave them alone.

But of course life wasn't like that.

'Then I might head back to the villa.'

'I thought you might say that.'

'Sebastián, the next time I'm here it will be with my daughter.'

How? Anna begged in her mind. *How can I ever see him and act casually? How can I begin to accept that we will never have this precious time again?*

No future, he had said. No falling in love.

'I don't want anyone knowing we had a…thing.'

'A thing?' Sebastián checked.

'A fling. A sex fest. A brief romance. I don't know what to call it, but I don't want to have to explain it to them.'

'Fine,' he snapped.

'One other thing…'

'Go on,' he prompted.

'The crew…'

His eyes narrowed. 'What about them?'

'At the celebration tomorrow…' She swallowed audibly. 'Well, Emily will think…they'll all think… it's my first time on the boat…'

'Yacht,' he corrected, in a pompous, arrogant tone. 'And my crew are *always* discreet.'

'Even so…' Anna thought of how friendly they were with her now, how they called her by name. 'Could you just have a word?'

'I'm not about to explain to my crew that you

wish what we have shared to remain a secret.' Sebastián shook his head. 'I can assure you that you will be greeted politely—as are all my guests.'

'Thank you.'

She stood there, feeling so uncertain because they were fighting—not shouting or even arguing... No, Anna corrected, she was fighting herself. Fighting not to admit to herself that it was very possible, or rather very likely, she was in L-O-V-E. She didn't even want to say the word to herself, because it spelt trouble. It was impossible...

'I'd better go.'

'Adios.'

No! Was that it? Was that all he was going to say? She wanted...

He glanced down as his phone bleeped and read the message. 'Carmen's just left the hospital, so she's ten minutes away.

Or six, the way the Romeros drove and left their cars half parked for others to deal with...or simply stepped out of a chauffeur-driven car.

She knew it wasn't really Carmen she was worried about confronting—it was her own heart. And if she stayed for even another moment she might say something she really regretted.

'I don't want them knowing because not everyone has the same attitude towards casual relationships,' Anna explained.

'I have *never* treated you casually.'

'I know that!'

'Good. So go and do what you have to do, and I shall spend time with my sister. *Adios.*'

No, no, no.

'When—?'

But she never got to finish asking when they would see each other because he interrupted.

'When what? Do you want me to text you when the coast is clear? Because that really would be crass.'

'What has changed all of a sudden?' Anna demanded.

'Nothing.'

'Something has. We used to talk—'

'Oh, please,' he broke in. 'We've been seeing each other for a matter of days. "Used to" is stretching it. You said you wanted a holiday…some fun. That was the deal.'

'The *deal*?' She gave an incredulous snort. 'Well, the deal's off—and, no, I don't want a text when the coast is clear.'

Good, he thought. *Now get out of my heart. Done.*

But not quite…

She turned and came right up to his face. 'Did I get too close?' she asked. 'Is that it?'

He said nothing.

'After all that, you can't even end it nicely.'

And with that, Anna left the yacht.

She couldn't bear the way it had all come about in the end. Despite the heat, she almost ran through the marina and towards the villa, and it felt as if the truth was chasing her the whole way. Demanding that she confront it.

Only when the door had closed behind her, as she stood in the cool, air-conditioned room, did she dare to admit it that she'd fallen head over heels with the…

'Bastard!'

She said it out loud.

Anna swore for the first time in her life.

She had been fighting the fact that she might love him since their first night together. For months it had been an easy battle. She'd just had to recall their awful first parting…or tell herself what a dreadful person he was by reading salacious gossip.

Then she'd spent days and nights being bathed in his kisses and his charm, and now he'd withdrawn it her heart felt as if was at war with itself.

Trying to hold back the truth was like trying to hold back the tide. She'd been warned. She'd been told. And she had no one to blame but herself.

She was utterly and deeply in love with Sebastián Romero.

Their row had delayed Anna's departure and Carmen arrived just a couple of moments later, but if she had seen Anna leave she said nothing to Sebastián.

'I can't stop,' she said, by way of greeting. 'Alejandro has asked me to take Anna out.'

'Again?'

'She wasn't there last time.' Carmen shrugged. 'So, what did you want?'

'To go over the arrangements for tomorrow—we're to meet at the hotel at...' He hesitated briefly. 'Five.'

'Okay.'

They chatted some more about the arrangements, but Carmen would give nothing away as to what was on her mind. If Anna hadn't spoken to him Sebastián knew he would still be none the wiser about what was troubling his sister.

Dios, he hated how things had ended with Anna. He knew full well he had pushed her away, because even if they were going nowhere Anna hadn't deserved what he had done.

He just did not know how to end things any other way.

She was right. Texting *would* be crass.

He would call her once Carmen had left.

Maybe he'd go over there...?

He should do the one thing she wished her ex had and end things nicely.

'I'd better call her,' Carmen said, picking up her phone. 'Anna! It's Carmen. Do you want to go out this evening?' She laughed. 'Get wildly drunk and dance the night away? See if there are *any* decent single men left out there?'

Sebastián couldn't help but smile at his sister.

'Okay,' Carmen said. 'I'll meet you there.'

He wasn't smiling now.

'I'm off,' Carmen said, and kissed her brother's cheek. 'Five o'clock tomorrow, yes?'

'Yes,' Sebastián said.

And a few hours later, when he checked his phone and saw his sister's latest social media update, there was Carmen…but also there was Anna, in her silver dress and heels…

There was no jealousy, just the knowledge that their row had hurt her and that she must be bleeding inside.

He knew that because he was too.

But he would not be pinning this butterfly and storing her in a display case. He wanted her to spread her wings, for she deserved more than just a sliver of him. She knew her worth and she would insist on a heart that could give.

'I got too close,' she had accused.

Too close, he quietly now agreed.

He'd come to admire her, and never more than on this night.

He raised his glass, and even smiled, because he knew how to put this a little bit right.

'Go, Anna!'

CHAPTER FIFTEEN

'WHERE'S CARMEN?' JOSÉ ASKED.

Sebastián shrugged. 'I told everyone four o'clock,' he said, even though he had told Carmen five.

He tried not to look over, but even in the periphery of his vision Anna Douglas made a stunning entrance.

She wore a lilac halter-neck dress and the flat sandals she'd arrived in. Her hair was up and she had dark glasses on.

Sebastián suppressed a smile. He knew from his sister's updates that it had been a very late night— or rather it had gone on well into the morning.

However, her eyes looked fine when she took her sunglasses off, and he watched those gorgeous green orbs sweep the gathering, feeling them linger a second on him.

He gave her a nondescript smile as she approached and left it to his brother to do the introductions 'You've met Anna, of course,' Alejandro said.

'Of course,' José said. 'At the wedding. Emily's friend. Yes?' His English was good, but not great.

'Yes.' Anna smiled. 'You must be looking forward to meeting your grandchild.'

'Very much,' Maria crooned. 'We're so excited—aren't we, darling?'

'You can only see her through the glass,' Sebastián warned. 'And only if she's well enough.'

'We don't care,' José said, squeezing Maria's hand, 'just so long as we get to see her.'

How it incensed him! Not his father—Maria. Inserting herself into the family as a doting grandmother, trying to gloss over the years of her absence.

'It is good that you have been here for Emily,' Maria said to Anna in a throaty voice. 'She needs a friend at a time like this. Poor thing…'

'Papá,' Sebastián interjected. He didn't want to hear feigned concern from his mother. 'Can we go for a walk? I want to speak with you. With us all away from the office, things are piling up.'

'Always business with you…' José grumbled.

'Can't we just keep it about family today?' Alejandro asked his brother.

'The world keeps turning,' Sebastián said. 'We can't all just take a month or three off.'

Sebastián didn't care if he came across as a cold-hearted devil. It was what they expected him to be. But he wanted to get his father on his own and work was the obvious excuse.

José, though, was rather more familiar with his eldest son's tactics, and as they stepped out into the bright son, he rolled his eyes.

'Don't worry. I know the baby is very small. I'm not going to—'

'It's not about the baby.'

'Well, I don't want to hear anything against your mother. She's excited to be here, and if you can't accept that—'

'It's not about Maria.' Sebastián signalled to a table at a café and the rope was removed so they could step in and take a seat. He ordered coffee for them both. 'Carmen is going to speak to you.'

'About?'

'Riding.'

'What about it?'

'She's unsure if it's what she wants to do with her life and—'

'Of *course* it's what she wants to do.'

'Listen—'

'No!' Jose thumped the table. 'She's world-class. It is what she loves.'

Sebastián sat and listened as his father gave every reason he had expected him to as to why Carmen shouldn't give it up.

'Finished?' he said.

'I have not finished. That girl doesn't know what she wants. This is the one thing she excels at!'

'Listen to me, Papá.' He leant forward and stared right into his father's eyes, as he had so very many times. 'She needs to know you love her—that whatever she does with her life she has your support.'

'Well, she doesn't in this,' José huffed. 'Why the hell would she give it up?'

Sebastián spooned sugar into his coffee and let him carry on. There was a certain feeling of déjà vu about this situation. Throughout Carmen's childhood and teenage years he had pre-warned or primed José, deciding it might be better for his at times fiery father to let off the inevitable steam with his eldest rather than with his sensitive and temperamental youngest.

'We should get back,' Sebastián said. 'Don't tell her I—'

'Okay, okay,' José snapped. 'I won't tell her you said anything.' They stopped for a moment and looked out at the yachts. 'Where's yours?'

Sebastián pointed. 'We're going there after the hospital.'

'It's been ages,' José said. 'And your mother has never been on board. It will be nice for her to see it.'

'Yes,' Sebastián said, not revealing the supreme effort behind that single word. He would have her walk the plank if he could, for all she had done— or rather not done. To Carmen and Alejandro too…

He glanced at his father, smiling as he looked out at the water, and for his sake kept his own emotions in check and joined in with his idle chit-chat.

'You still have Dante as the captain?'

'Of course.' Sebastián nodded. 'He'll be pleased to welcome you.'

The cars were all ready and Carmen had arrived by the time they got back.

'You said we were meeting at five!' she accused.

'The cars are at five. You were to be here at four.'

Anna stood a little apart from everyone, and

when Alejandro guided her into a car, he pointed to a different one for Sebastián.

It was a difficult day for so many reasons, yet there was so much happiness too as they all stood looking through the glass at the newest addition to their family. The incubator had been moved closer to the window, and Sebastián heard José's cry of delight at the sight of his granddaughter.

Even Maria, who lacked a single maternal bone in her body, let out a sob when she saw the tiny girl. 'Oh, *bebita*…' she crooned. 'She needs a name, Alejandro.'

'I think she might have one,' Sebastián said.

For although he was mildly enthralled with his niece, his sharp eyes had been drawn to the embroidered blanket that had been carefully hung over the incubator. The machinery on view was softened by it, and there on the delicately embroidered blanket was the date of her birth and the tiny little girl's name: *Josefa Romero Jacobs*.

'Josefa,' Sebastián said, pronouncing it *Hosefa*. 'The female for José.'

He looked quickly back to the baby as his father started to cry—a familiar sound and one he had hated all his life. But he reminded himself that today these were happy tears.

Even though to him they sounded the same as the ones from his childhood.

'Anna made it,' Emily told the little gathering.

'It's taken her months. She added the name this week.'

'You surely didn't have her sewing on her holiday?' Maria sounded appalled at the notion, and for once she almost put a smile on her eldest son's face.

He had known, of course, that Anna had a secret, but her hiding something and returning to the villa occasionally made better sense now.

He had to fight not to turn his head and give Anna a smile…not to put his arm around her and pull her in and compliment her work. He had to stand still and not react. Because if he did, then he would break his word to her.

He would also be revealing something of himself. Because he did not do affection, or handholding, or anything of the sort. Not in public, and up until now not really in private either.

He could hear the sound of his father's tears as he looked at his tiny granddaughter. 'Josefa…' he kept saying, over and over.

Sebastián stared ahead as Emily gently told the fragile man that they had asked permission for him to hold the baby. 'Alejandro has given up his turn this afternoon.'

'Oh.' Maria sighed excitedly. 'Please let me hold her!'

'Just Papá,' Alejandro said. 'She's too little to be passed around.'

'But surely just one little cuddle…?' Maria pouted.

Now Sebastián turned around. 'Just Papá.'

Anna blinked at the tone in Sebastián's voice.

It wasn't loud, or harsh, or anything like that, but it was still the sound of a final decision.

One with which no one would argue.

She couldn't help but wonder if he was being a bit harsh on his mother. She was attention-seeking, yes, but she'd been kind about Emily—and José did seem thrilled and deeply in love with his wife.

'We'll go to the waiting room,' he said now, and put his hand on his father's shoulder. 'Congratulations, Papá…'

It was a private moment for José, so Anna went into the waiting room along with Sebastián and Carmen—who was still smarting that her mother was present at all.

'"Oh, *bebita*",' she mimicked savagely, and then translated for Anna. 'It means baby girl. I doubt she was so overcome when she saw *me*.'

'Carmen!' Sebastián said.

Anna could hear the strain in his voice, and perhaps wisely he chose not to debate the topic right now.

'Let's just try for one good night, shall we?' he suggested, and then took out his phone. 'I'll let Dante know we'll be aboard soon.'

It was only when Carmen huffed off to stare out of the window that he finally met Anna's eyes.

He gave her a half-smile—or a quarter-smile and a tiny nod—and she quickly turned her head away, because she didn't know how they were after the way things had ended between them.

'How was your night with Carmen?' he asked.

'Fun!' she said brightly.

But when she met his gaze her eyes filled with tears, because she loathed the pettiness of revenge and that was what last night had been for her.

She'd stuck to sparkling water all night, but she'd laughed and danced as if she was a glamorous and single twenty-something with no responsibilities, having the time of her life on a starry night in Puerto Banús.

She wished that she'd simply curled up and cried instead.

He gave her another smile and that made her feel even worse.

When they were finished at the hospital the cars were ready to take them to the marina, and she sat with Alejandro and Emily, who was obviously nervous at leaving her tiny baby in the hospital.

'She'll be fine,' she told her friend.

'I know,' Emily said.

'How was José when he held her?' Anna asked.

'So proud,' Emily said, and she showed her a couple of photos on her phone.

That reminded Anna of something. 'I have to

take some photos of us,' she said. 'Willow keeps asking for more.'

'We'll get some on the yacht,' Emily said. 'How is she?'

'They're driving back from Scotland today. She's starting to miss me and…' A lump filled her throat but she squashed it down, and Emily squeezed her hand.

'Thanks for being here,' she said. 'And I am so sorry for asking you to do that blanket. I wasn't thinking…'

'It nearly killed me!' Anna laughed.

They began to walk along the jetty towards the yacht. Maria's flamenco shoes were clipping loudly and drawing the eyes of all around.

'Maria de Luca!' someone called out, and she smiled and waved and blew kisses with the hand that wasn't holding José's.

Emily and Alejandro were holding hands too, and Carmen was casually checking her phone. Sebastián walked ahead alone and Anna ached to walk beside him, sensing this night was incredibly hard for him.

His yacht had never looked more beautiful, Anna thought as they made their way towards it. In a sea of white, it was softly lit pink in the dusky night and she felt a little foolish for having asked Sebastián to warn the crew, because they were, of course, impeccable.

'Bienvenido a bordo, Señor Romero.'

José was welcomed back warmly, and Dante greeted all the other guests by name.

'Señorita de Luca.'

He welcomed Maria courteously, and in Spanish asked her to remove her shoes. Anna was back to being *señorita*, as she had been the first night she had been here.

'Can I ask that you…?' He gestured to her shoes and to the basket.

Carmen had already taken hers off and was heading up onto deck.

'Of course,' Anna said, and leant on the wall to remove her shoes, trying not to recall all the tender times Sebastián had done this for her.

'Señorita de Luca?'

The *capitán* was calling Maria back. Clearly, Anna thought, she hadn't heard his request, because she was still wearing her shoes.

'*Por favor?*' He was politely insistent.

Anna felt her heart still as Maria shot the *capitán* a look so dark and fierce that Anna sensed a shiver on her neck before her heart suddenly beat faster.

No wonder Sebastián was so protective of his family. This was her first glimpse of Maria with her mask off—though of course she quickly snapped it back on and returned to being 'Grandmother of the Year' as she complied.

'*Por supuesto,*' she said, but insolently, and she

did not put her shoes in the basket. Instead she left them lying in a heap on the floor.

'*Gracias*, Señorita De Luca.' Dante smiled his perfect smile.

He really was a true *capitán*!

Anna was honestly a bit shaken, but either the others hadn't noticed or they were used to it, because no comment was made.

Emily gasped when she arrived on deck. There were tiny arrangements of soft pink daisies and pink candles, and champagne corks were popping. Little Josefa's arrival was being properly celebrated.

'It's so nice to taste fresh air,' Emily said. 'Gosh, what a week…'

Anna caught Sebastián's eyes, very briefly, and she was proud of them both as they gave nothing away.

She thought of the future—years from now, perhaps. When he might be celebrating…whatever. Sebastián, old on his yacht and too rich to be lonely…

I ought to take some pictures, she thought.

She took a few of Emily and Alejandro, and of the cake when it came out. Delicate layers of pastry layered with pink jam and white chocolate ganache…

Sebastián had done all this. Or the crew, perhaps. But she had heard his meetings with Dante and the chef, and knew of the effort he'd made…

'To Josefa!' Sebastián said, and everyone clinked their glasses.

'Willow would have loved this,' Emily said. 'You'll have to take some cake back for her.'

'She'll love it!' Anna smiled.

Alejandro handed out cards for everyone, with photos of the new baby, and Anna found she had to excuse herself. She was tearful and trying not to be, missing being here already, and daunted at the prospect of leaving it all behind.

And that dreadful ending…

Anna was looking up at the stars and the rising moon, and wondering if her phone's camera was up to it, when she heard Carmen.

'I mean it!' She sounded adamant. 'I'm thinking of taking a break. Maybe travelling…'

'Come off it!' Alejandro said. 'As if anything would tear you away from the horses.'

'Why would you give up now?' Sebastián asked.

Anna held her breath, surprised by the harsh question when she'd told him how sensitive this topic was.

'An athlete is only at the top of their game for a small window of time,' he went on.

'Hey!' José interrupted his eldest son. 'If Carmen wants a break then she has earnt one. Whatever she does, we support her.'

'Papá!' Carmen let out a shriek of laughter and moved from her seat to kiss his cheek, and Anna smiled as José pulled her onto his knee.

The family were all together, and she held up her phone, wondering whether or not she should capture an image of it. Most certainly she could do it unobtrusively, and so she snapped a quick photo of the 'Elusive Five'. She knew from Emily that there were hardly any pictures of the five of them.

And then she turned back to the gorgeous night.

But all too soon it was over.

Presents were being handed out by Dante—little flamenco dolls holding Spanish sweets—and Anna just knew Willow would love one.

'Plastic Flamenco dolls!' Maria said, derisively. 'They're a bit touristy! Did you choose these, Alejandro?'

'I chose them,' Sebastián responded tartly responded. 'I'm not exactly up on baby celebrations and Alejandro has been busy.'

He caught her eyes then and Anna smiled. She knew he had somehow chosen the perfect gift to give Willow when she broke the news of the baby to her daughter.

'Well, I think it's gorgeous,' she spoke up for him. 'I'm going to give Willow mine.'

'Take two,' Sebastián said.

And that was it.

The end of their time.

Her heart was lost.

There were effusive goodbyes, with José hugging Emily and Alejandro, and Maria too. Sebastián gave his father a kiss, but as Maria moved to kiss her son he turned his cheek just enough that it missed.

Maria noticed.

Anna did too.

But for the rest it was a friendly goodbye.

'I'll see you next time, Anna.' Carmen smiled and kissed her new friend goodbye. 'Or maybe in England? We'll go raving!'

'Thank you for being here,' José said, and hugged her.

Anna turned and knew it was time to bid farewell to Sebastián. She just didn't know how to, and was pathetically grateful when her phone rang.

'Oh, excuse me. It's my daughter.'

She removed herself to take it, and chatted to Willow, who was happy but also desperate for it to be tomorrow so she could see her mum.

'One more sleep,' Anna said. 'I can't wait to see you. I've missed you so much.'

In the background she heard Sebastián speaking.

'I'll see that Anna gets back,' Sebastián said. 'You go straight to the hospital.'

'We can wait,' Alejandro said, despite his obvious eagerness to get back to his baby.

'Anna will be fine,' Sebastián insisted. 'Go and see your baby.'

'Come on,' Alejandro said to his wife. 'Sebastián says he will see that Anna gets back.'

'Tell her we'll have breakfast tomorrow.'

'For sure.'

Anna waved to her friend, and then turned her attention back to Willow, grateful to Sebastián for engineering some time for them to say goodbye privately.

The crew were clearing up, but he had a word and they melted away, and as she ended her call the cabin felt incredibly quiet.

'Peace at last,' Sebastián said.

'They are rather loud,' Anna agreed.

'I meant between us.'

'Oh…' She took a breath. 'Peace?'

'We can do better than last night, can't we?'

Yes, they could.

He poured her a fresh glass of champagne and they sat on one of the sofas. Conversation was a little awkward as they began an attempt to redefine their relationship as friends.

'Today was beautiful,' Anna said.

'It went as well as it could. Thank goodness I kept it short.'

'Your father was great with Carmen.'

'Yes.'

She didn't understand why he'd snapped at his sister when she'd told him how sensitive Carmen was about things, but she let it go, just pleased it had worked out.

'And José got to hold the baby.'

'Maria thought it should be her,' Sebastián said, rolling his eyes.

Anna frowned and felt her arms goosebump. 'She was a little jealous.'

'She disappeared for twenty-five years and yet

thinks she should hold her grandchild before my father!'

'They do seem happy,' she attempted, out of politeness, but then she recalled *that* look from Maria, and knew he wasn't being harsh in his judgement.

'For now.'

He gave a low, scoffing laugh, but Anna knew it wasn't aimed at her.

'Until she changes her mind.'

'You don't think she'll leave?'

'I think she came back because we thought he only had a few weeks to live. That changed after he had his surgery. I don't know how long he's got now. I just hope it's longer than her attention span.'

'Why would she be by his side if she didn't love him?'

He didn't answer.

'Is it for the money?' Anna asked. 'Or because she wants to be sure she remains part of the brand?'

'Both, in part.' Sebastián didn't soften. 'But it's more that she wants to be his widow, and wear black, and walk behind his coffin. Be the recipient of all the attention she craves.'

'You don't think she loves him?'

'I believe she's incapable of loving anyone other than herself.'

Anna sat there and tried to take it in, stunned. Then she looked at his serious expression and wondered how bad his relationship with his mother must have been for him to draw such a conclusion.

'I saw the look she gave Dante when he asked her to remove her shoes,' she said.

'I know that look well,' he nodded.

'What was life like for you?'

Sebastián didn't answer that one. He shook his head. 'Enough about her. How's Willow?'

'Desperate for me to get home.'

'She misses you?'

'Yes.'

'Emily wants you to see her for breakfast tomorrow.'

'I heard.'

'You're in demand.'

'Yes.'

'With me too.'

'It doesn't feel like it,' Anna said, and then she looked right at him. 'Thank you, Sebastián.'

It felt imperative to say this now, before the emotion of leaving rendered her unable to say it without breaking down. She did not want to end the most perfect week of her life with tears.

'It's been wonderful.' She gave a small, wistful smile. 'All of it. Well…' She looked over. 'Apart from last night. I'm sorry I went off dancing with Carmen.'

'Anna, it was the best thing you could have done. You need to get out dancing more.'

'I wish we'd been able to talk it out.'

'We can now.' He looked at her. 'If we're both honest.'

'Something changed?'

'Yes,' he admitted.

'When Carmen came by the first time.'

'No.'

'Yes,' Anna insisted.

'Yes,' he conceded. 'She told me something about you wanting more children and to settle down, and it freaked me out.'

'I said all that to get her to open up. I said that before you came back. Before we were together.'

'It's true, though?'

'One day.' She nodded. 'Maybe. But I don't get why something I said to Carmen—'

'It changed before that, Anna.'

'No…'

'Anna.' He was both gentle and firm. 'In the water, what were you going to say?'

She shook her head. 'I don't want say it now.'

'Fair enough, but you know we were getting in too deep.'

'Only because you made it that way.'

'Do you want me to look you up when I come to England now and then? Maybe sneak away for a few days when you come to visit Emily?'

'I don't know.' She shook her head. 'Maybe.'

'No.' He shook his head. 'You want more than that for your future. So do I. And I don't want us to get closer only for you to…'

'To what?'

'Come on, Anna. You've done the tough part.

Willow will soon be going to school. You're going to start the career you want. You're not going to settle for some occasional catch-up with a guy in Spain.'

He might as well have got a pen and written on the table before them in capital letters: I DON'T WANT YOUR LOVE.

And there was no point arguing with that.

'You're right.' She sniffed, and then nodded. 'I do want more than that. But not yet…'

She didn't want it to be over, but knew it was.

'We end it now,' Sebastián said. 'Nicely.'

'Yes…'

'You've got a family waiting at home who love you.' He must have seen her eyebrows rise. 'They do,' he said. 'It's time to forgive yourself for hurting them. Just be yourself.'

'I don't even know who that is,' Anna admitted, because this week had spun her around, and she felt as if her heart lived in two worlds.

'*I* do,' Sebastián said. 'And she's actually very nice. I know, because I've spent a week with her.' He gave her a smile. 'It was fun. Here…' He reached beneath the table. 'I got you a gift.'

'Please don't…'

'Why? Don't you like gifts?'

'I do but…' The dark brown box he handed her already told her it was too much. Now she was almost crying. 'I can't take this…'

'Open it.'

What she saw made her gasp.

It was a beautiful white gold Fabergé egg pendant.

'I got a long chain,' he said. 'Everyone will think it's just a necklace.'

'Nobody would think this was "just a necklace".'

It was so exquisite—the detailing, the absolute beauty of the design...

'Open it,' he said.

Anna frowned, not sure what he meant, but then she realised the egg had a catch. When she opened it, she saw that inside was a tiny yacht.

'Oh!'

She had never been one for gifts and had loathed the thought of him giving her an expensive present, but the little secret yacht was perfection. And he was right—no one even needed to see beyond the chain.

She took a breath and was honest. 'I love it. It's so beautiful...'

'Like you.'

He took it out of the box and smoothed back her hair, lifting it away from her neck. She felt the cool weight of the egg nestle between her breasts as he fastened the clasp. It was the most romantic gift—a little time capsule of their week together that she could wear, or put away and just take out sometimes...

'Thank you, Sebastián.' She leant in and kissed

him lightly, feeling his warm lips on hers, and then the slide of his tongue.

She would never understand how he could kiss her in a way that felt so close to the perfect good-bye…how he could take her by the hand down to his cabin…

His suite was exquisite, the most private place on the yacht, the closest she could ever get to the centre of his world, and here he kissed her as if they weren't saying goodbye…as if he loved her.

And Anna kissed him back with deep passion… because she loved him.

He removed the straps from her shoulders and slid down her dress. 'You look…'

He took in the changes their week had made, the white breasts where her bikini had stayed firmly on. They made him smile, and as his hand dusted over her nipples and then stroked her stomach she closed her eyes to the sensation.

'Sunkissed,' was his verdict.

She was *Sebastián*-kissed, she corrected mentally. Because it wasn't just the sun that had wreaked changes in Anna. It was a week of being made love to, of moments lying together on a beach or in bed, or on a lounger, just talking,

All she had missed out on in life so far he had given her in spades. And yet, selfishly perhaps, for Anna it still wasn't enough.

He kissed her breasts as he pulled her in, and then kissed her stomach as he slid down her knickers.

His breathing was heavy and her eyelashes fluttered closed as she anticipated what was to come.

One soft kiss, sweeter than any delicacy, and then he moved in for more.

Anna gave a soft moan as she fell back on plump pillows. She could smell his cologne and the sun on his shirt. She allowed herself to inhale and breathe in the pleasure as he kissed her neck and then said words in Spanish that sounded a lot like how she felt.

He took her flushed face in his hands and gave her slow, wet kisses that weakened her. He climbed on top of her and parted her legs. He couldn't know how she physically ached for him to enter her.

'Sebastián...'

He was still half dressed, but she didn't care. And he was unsheathed, but she cared even less about that. She just had to have him inside her.

But he stopped to sheathe himself.

Always.

They'd both been burned before.

And yet there was a stab of regret—or realisation, perhaps—but then, as he kissed her hard, he dragged her back to that blurry place where details didn't matter. And he was entering her, and driving in, and she had never known such tender loving as he took every moment of their time together and condensed it into this.

Anna kissed him as she wanted to—as if it was for ever and this wasn't their final night. Their eyes locked he moved within her, but then she turned her head and looked away—because she had to.

She felt as if she were giving herself to him entirely, but even as her body rippled with pleasure she knew that he held himself back.

'Don't…' she said, but she didn't know quite what she was telling him.

She sank again, dragged back to oblivion as his tempo increased. His shout as he came was almost silent, breathless, but it reverberated through her, summoning her, and she felt the clench of every cell as she gave in to him. Just caved…

It was afterwards, as she lay there, the blur fading, that she knew for certain he had held back. Despite her willingness, and being on the Pill, still he'd sheathed.

Slivers of his heart was all he'd ever give.

He took care of the details, never trusting anyone else to.

He would never get that close to someone.

He didn't trust her…

Probably he never would.

CHAPTER SIXTEEN

ANNA WOKE BEFORE him and realised it was to the sound of his phone.

The buzzing faded and she found she did not know what to do. Should she simply get dressed and leave quietly, without saying goodbye?

Perhaps ending things nicely wasn't the best way after all...

Anger had felt easier to navigate than being sent off nicely with presents and best wishes...

Don't end it on a row, Anna warned herself. *Or with tears!*

Then his phone buzzed again, and his first word on waking was a swear word.

'Sebastián!' she exclaimed, and actually laughed at how incompatible they were. And then she met his lovely black eyes. 'It really is time for me to go. I'm starting to nag!'

'You can nag for a couple more hours,' he said, pulling her towards him and obliterating thought with his scratchy morning jaw—until his blessed phone buzzed again.

It was Anna who almost swore this time.

'I'd better get this.'

He rolled away from her and reached for his phone as Anna lay there, her eyes determinedly closed.

It wasn't a shout that had her opening her eyes.

Instead it was a low, husky whisper that was pure anguish.

'Dios, no!' Sebastián said.

She shot to attention.

She could hear screams coming down the phone, and Sebastián saying *'Cálmate...'* clearly telling the caller to calm down.

Anna sat up, her first thought that something must have happened to the baby. She tried to stand, to reach for her clothes, to go to her friend, but then his hand came to her arm and he stroked it lightly, giving a slight shake of his head which somehow reassured her.

He'd done the same at the airport, Anna recalled. Even though they'd been barely talking, he'd seen her anguish and reassured her with his touch, with his eyes, before he'd even spoken.

And he did the same now, stroking her arm as he spoke in rapid Spanish for a couple of moments before ending the call.

What's wrong? It was the obvious question to ask. *What's happened?*

Yet they would be such pointless questions when clearly he was too stunned to answer. So instead of asking she watched as he stood there, naked, as if still taking it in. He proceeded to sit on the bed, and she watched the phone slip from his hand and fall to the floor as he put his head in his hands.

'My father...' he said.

She swallowed.

'That was Maria. They were—' He shook his head. 'I think they were making love.'

'Oh, Sebastián…'

'An ambulance and a doctor came, but no…' He shook his head. 'He's gone.'

Sometimes there were no words, so Anna knelt and put her hand on his shoulder, felt his rapid, shallow breaths.

'Carmen's hysterical,' he said, more to himself than to Anna. 'I knew he was sick, and we all knew this day was coming, but not yet…'

And then he took a shaky breath and his head went down into his hands. It felt as if the biggest, strongest tree was giving way beneath her fingers.

It was a very private moment that she was certain he would prefer no one to see. He let out a couple of low sobs and she could see his fingers pressed into his eyes. She didn't know what to do, or how to comfort him, so she just hugged him tightly. Perhaps it was the right thing, because he brought her to his lap and it was like watching the sun go down to see the tears falling from his eyes.

'Not yet,' he said, and she clung to him. 'I thought he had more time.' He looked at her then. Right at her, as if they were in that deep water again, as if their souls were locked together. 'Will you please stay? I can't imagine the funeral…'

'Sebastián!' Her mouth gaped and Anna felt her heart split down the middle, torn completely in two. She really didn't know what to say or do.

He spoke before she could. 'You can't.' He said it for her. 'I know. I forgot for a moment that you leave today.'

'I have to get back to Willow.'

'Of course.'

He retracted his question immediately, that brief glimpse of his agony wiped away as he tipped her off his knee and went back to being the strongest tree, all signs of vulnerability erased.

'Of course you do,' he said. 'You must go—and so must I. I have so much to do.'

'I know.'

Anna sat there, hugging her knees, as he took the quickest shower and then dressed hurriedly, calling his PA as he did so, to arrange an urgent flight from Marbella to Jerez. If she didn't know better, she might think he was getting ready for work.

'I have to get to the hospital and tell Alejandro. Carmen's probably calling him now, but I asked her to wait and let me tell him face to face.'

He closed his eyes for a brief second and she saw it then—how he dealt with it all, and probably had since he was ten years old. Before that, even.

Wow.

She watched him snap back into business mode and she saw then why they called him tough—he had to be. Because everything came to him, everyone looked to him, all worries landed on his shoulders. Now he was on the phone again, speaking with whom she did not know, but it sounded like a priest.

Then he paused, kissed her cheek, 'I really do have to—'

'I know.'

'Stay as long as you—'

'I can sort myself out.' She gave a shaky smile. 'Worry about yourself and your family. I'm so sorry, Sebastián.' As he threw things into a small case she hurriedly took out her phone. 'I took this photo of you all last night.'

'I haven't got time—'

'It's of the five of you,' Anna said. 'It might help, if you would like it?' she attempted.

But he was heading out through the door.

'It doesn't matter.'

Last night seemed to have taken place in a whole other world, and everything in this one was suddenly different. It was her last morning in Puerto Banús, and breakfast was served on the deck of the yacht, but she could barely manage the coffee.

It felt wrong to be on the outside.

She felt as if she should be there, with the rest of the family, but it was she herself who had demanded that they remain a secret.

Emily called an hour or so later and told Anna the news she already knew.

'How's Alejandro?' asked Anna.

'Stunned,' Emily said. 'He's flying back to Jerez now, with Sebastián.'

'Do you want me to come to the hospital?'

'Please…'

Emily was in a little suite attached to the NICU. It was a place that was used to hearing bad news— but not of an old, sick man dying.

It was still devastating…

'Do you know when the funeral is?' Anna asked.

'Sebastián is sorting it—but probably tomorrow.'

'So soon?'

'They take place much more quickly here.'

'Will you go?'

'I don't know.' Emily gave a helpless shake of her head. 'I don't know how I can be so far away from Josefa when she's so small.' She looked at her friend. 'But I know you have to go back. I understand that more than ever now.'

'I haven't seen Willow in over a week. My mother…'

'I know things are still shaky there. We'll be fine,' Emily said. 'I mean, it's not about me, is it? It's about Alejandro.'

And for Anna it was about Sebastián.

He'd asked her to stay.

To be there for the funeral.

He didn't want for ever, and yet he'd wanted her presence on the most awful day.

How could she stay, though? Her mother would never accept the excuse that she wanted to stay for her friend's father-in-law's funeral. And anyway, Willow needed her…

Nothing would keep her from her daughter. Nothing came before that love. Anna had decided that long ago.

Yet things were different now.

There wasn't a rival for her love for her daughter.

But there *was* someone else in her life whom she loved too.

And even if there could never be a future for them, Anna knew she might be able to help him a little now, just by being there.

It was surprisingly easy to call her mother…

'We're just heading to church,' said Jean. 'Willow's ever so excited that you're coming—'

'Mother,' Anna cut in, 'can you take this call away from Willow, please? I need to speak to you.'

She heard her mother talking to Willow. 'I'm just going to check if Grandpa's got his service notes.'

There was the sound of heavy breathing and she could hear her mother climbing the stairs. And suddenly it dawned on Anna that this was what Sebastián had done when he'd asked his father to join him on a walk.

Everyone had accused him of putting work first, yet she could see now that he'd been getting his father away before Carmen joined them.

José's perfect response to his daughter had been orchestrated by Sebastián, Anna was sure of it. Because that was what he did. He had smoothed the way for his little sister, made sure her relationship with her father was protected, taken care of his family in ways they didn't even realise.

She was determined to be there for him now. Anna wasn't even nervous to speak with her mother. It was simply the right thing to do.

'Is the baby okay?' Jean asked.

'The baby's doing well,' Anna said. 'The thing is, Emily's father-in-law died this morning.'

'He's been ill for a while, hasn't he?'

'Yes, but it was still sudden and unexpected, though.'

'Okay...'

'Mum, I think I need to be here for the funeral—'

'Anna,' Jean cut in. 'I know Emily's going through a difficult time, but Willow's so looking forward—'

'This isn't about Emily.'

There was a very long silence. Her mother was waiting, and Anna was unsure how to formulate what she wanted to say, but it was more than that. It was also what she wanted—no, *needed* to happen next.

'Can I ask you to bring Willow out here to Marbella?'

'Marbella?' Her mother gave an incredulous laugh.

'I want to go the funeral and—'

'I'm sorry for their loss, but your daughter has to come first, surely?'

'She does,' Anna said, and took a breath. 'Mum, I've met someone… Alejandro's brother.' She knew that by voicing it she was opening herself up to hurt, and to her mother's scorn, but she was determined to do it anyway. 'He wants me here for the funeral and—'

'Someone you've known for a *week*?'

'We met at the wedding.'

'And was that why you flew off to Spain the first chance you got?'

'No!' She gave the Spanish *no*—the terse no… the absolute no. 'I'm not sure what's happening between us. I just know that I care about him very much, and now his father has died suddenly.' She did care very much, and there was a part of her that knew he cared too. 'We can't ever be a couple, but I can be a support to him. But I also need Willow—and she needs me.'

'I'm not just jumping on a plane with her to meet Mummy's latest—'

'That's uncalled for!' Anna snapped. 'Nothing will ever come before Willow, but she's old enough to know that her mother has a friend who's lost someone—'

'I'm sorry. No.'

'I understand,' Anna said—and perhaps she finally did. Her mother was entitled to her own opinions, but so too was Anna. She was entitled to make her own decisions and her own mistakes, and now she would make her own choices. 'I'll be home this afternoon as arranged, then, and I'll bring Willow back here myself.'

'You can't afford to do that.'

Anna couldn't afford not to. She had to listen to her heart…

It was all a little chaotic.

She booked the flights, and called Emily, and did all she could to put plans in place on her way back to England, so that by the time she walked into the vicarage she knew exactly what was happening.

'Mummy!'

Willow was the most incredible child—funny, and a bit of a show-off, wearing a tartan beret and full of smiles.

There were presents to be exchanged—Scottish rock for Anna, and the flamenco doll with sweets for Willow…

And a frosty catch-up with her parents.

When they were back in their own home, she told Willow about Josefa. And because she was only four—almost five—Willow didn't need exact details. She was simply excited to see the pictures.

'She's so cute! I want to hold her…'

'We can't hold her at the moment,' Anna said. 'Just her parents…'

And she thought of José, and how extra-precious that cuddle with his granddaughter was now.

'Willow, darling…' She took a deep breath. 'I have a friend in Spain and his father has just died.

It was ever so sudden. I think I ought to go to the funeral, so I can help him.'

'You're going back?' Her daughter's eyes widened in horror.

'With *you*!'

That quickly put a smile on her face.

'Emily's going to look after you, and she's finding a nanny to help her, as I might have to stay away overnight. But we'll have a couple of days together afterwards.'

'Where are we going?'

'It's a place called Marbella.'

Willow jumped up and down at the prospect of a plane ride, and seeing Emily, going to Spain…

'Will I get to see the baby?'

'Well…' Anna took a breath. She felt as if she was balancing on a tightrope. 'It depends… But you'll definitely be with Emily. She's desperate to see you.'

'Is there a beach?'

'Yes, there's a beach.' Anna smiled.

And it was at that very beach the next morning that she and her daughter found Emily.

'Willow!'

Emily hugged her goddaughter fiercely, and didn't let on anything about the difficulties she had been through, nor ask any of the questions she had for Willow's mother. She just chatted away and introduced Dali, a highly trained nanny, who was going to help take care of Willow.

Anna insisted on paying Dali herself, even if it meant she would have to dip into her precious emergency fund. If this wasn't an emergency, she didn't know what was.

Yes, it was going to be a juggling act just to get to the funeral, but Anna did everything she could to make it easy on her daughter, answering all Dali's questions about her Willow's likes and dislikes.

Then she faced a barrage of questions from her friend, when Dali took Willow to play on the gorgeous sand—she wanted to be sure Willow was comfortable with Dali before leaving them together.

'Dali's incredible,' Emily reassured her. 'I asked the nurses at the NICU, and they recommended her. We're going to stay at the hotel next to the hospital, and Dali will take care of Willow when I need to go in…'

Anna knew she could not put off Emily's questions any longer. She really had done everything she could to help when Anna had called, even if she was uncertain what she was doing was wise.

'I thought something was going on with you and Sebastián at the wedding…' she said.

'I know…'

'Why didn't you tell me?'

'I didn't need to be warned again,' Anna admitted.

'He did everything he could to break Alejandro

and me up. He got rid of me without thought, and I don't want the same thing to happen to you. It *hurt*.'

'I know… But he's hurting now,' Anna said. 'And I know we're going nowhere, but he's made me so happy. I can't tell you… This isn't about the future, or whether there's a chance for us. It's just the right thing to do.'

She gave her friend a smile.

'What happens when you come to visit me in a few months and he's seeing someone else?' asked Emily.

'I'll expect that,' Anna admitted. 'And I'm not going to let it make things awkward for the two of us, I promise. Have you told Alejandro?'

'What? That my usually sensible friend has gone completely crazy?' She gave a smile and then shook her head. 'No, I haven't told him. I was hoping to talk you out of going to the funeral.'

'Yet you found Dali?'

'I did…'

'Thank you.'

'You'd better hurry and catch your train…'

'How is Josefa?' Sebastián asked his brother.

'She is doing well.'

'She's a fighter.'

'Yes.'

'And Emily?'

'She has to stay there.'

'Of course.'

No question—Sebastián knew that.

He harboured no bitterness towards Anna for returning home. He knew, despite his first thoughts and that dreadful row, that she was a woman who was a mother first.

Unlike his.

And he admired her for it.

'I can't bear it…' Maria was weeping and waving *aromáticas* under her nose—but had managed to be in full make-up and funeral regalia.

Her day of days, Sebastián thought darkly.

But then he looked closely at his mother, and at her hands that shook as she tried to open her fan. Who was he, after all, to sit as judge and jury on love?

A dreadful mother? Yes.

An absent wife? True.

Yet José Romero's ending was the one his father would have chosen over any other, Sebastián knew.

'Here.' He handed his mother a small sherry and she nodded gratefully.

'This could be last time I'll see my photo on the bottle…' She sighed. 'You'll have every trace of me removed.'

'Let's not do this today,' Sebastián suggested firmly. 'Carmen needs—'

'Can everyone stop worrying about Carmen for a moment? *I* have just lost my husband.'

Dios, but he had to bite his tongue.

He looked at his sister, curled up in a chair, and truly wondered if she would make it through the day.

She was fragile, and she had not yet found out that the home she'd grown up in had been left to Maria. The land, the stables—all left to Maria too.

Sebastián would tell her tonight.

'I was always sniping at him…' his sister said now.

'No,' Sebastián said. 'Carmen, think of the wedding, and dancing with him. Think of that last night and how you two laughed…'

Perhaps he should text Anna and ask for that photo she had mentioned…but he dared not contact her today.

The funeral procession from home was slow as it meandered past the vines, and he watched as Carmen leant on Alejandro and sobbed.

They had always been close.

Really, he had never been close to anyone. Perhaps he was more like his mother than he would like?

Incapable of love.

He looked at Maria's black eyes and intact mascara and eyeliner. From knowing Anna, he found he actually understood his mother less.

Every night and morning Anna had called her daughter. She had spoken about her, thought about her, put her needs first…

And he wished, more than he dared admit, that she could be here today.

The hearse had stopped, so that the family could walk the last few steps to the church behind the coffin.

Sebastián checked that his sister was ready, that Maria was not fainting dramatically, and told his brother to get off the damn phone to his wife.

Then, as he watched the coffin being slid out of the hearse, he stood ramrod-straight.

He tried to do the right thing and took his mother's elbow…

She brushed it off.

Maria de Luca would make her entrance solo.

More dramatic that way, he thought bitterly.

And then, on this, the darkest of days, he saw a blonde head, and the one face he needed to see was there in the crowd.

'Anna?' he whispered, frowning.

Sebastián stepped out of the line and walked over to her.

'I thought you went home?'

'I did. I had to. But you asked… I thought it might help…'

Her lips were as white as marble, and there were black rings under her eyes—no doubt from back-to-back flights.

'If there's anything I can do…? I think they're calling for you.'

The procession into the church was about to start.

'Why did you come?' His brain was moving slowly. 'In place of Emily?'

'For *you*,' Anna said. 'I wanted to be here for you.'

That was it, he realised as he gave a slightly bewildered nod and headed back to join his siblings.

Anna was here without agenda.

She had made no demands.

She stood in the crowd outside the church, simply to be there.

For him.

'Walk with me,' he said.

He saw her swallow.

'Be with me today.'

'Okay…'

Even if they never shared another kiss, another night, another anything, it was, she knew, the right thing to have done.

One night.

One week.

No regrets.

He was not a demonstrative man in public. There was no hand-holding or anything. To all and sundry she might well be a cousin by his side, but what mattered was that she was *there*…

'Por qué está aquí?' his mother asked, and more from the tone than the words Anna knew Maria was asking what she was doing there.

Sebastián answered in English. 'Nothing you would understand.'

It was his one slight dig—not that his mother noticed. But she would not—*could* not understand that Anna, no matter the difficulty, had done everything she could to be here for him.

She was beside him during the service, and then afterwards, back at the bodega. She had not expected to return here so soon—and certainly not under such sad circumstances.

'I have to go and accept condolences,' Sebastián explained. 'Can we speak later?'

'Just do what you have to do,' Anna said.

On the stage there was a huge photo of José. The restaurant tables were pushed to one side and there were candles burning in the alcoves and beautiful flowers everywhere. Yet despite the stunning surroundings there was volatile edge to the mood, as if the black sherry barrels were kegs of gunpowder that at any moment might ignite.

Carmen was a mess, and Alejandro was pale and haggard—which was hardly surprising after the week he'd had. Maria looked fabulous and was graciously accepting condolences and fanning herself.

And then there was Sebastián.

He shook hands, smiled politely and said all the right things to the right people. Yet she could see the tension in his shoulders, the muscle leaping in his cheek. Even the tendons in his neck were tightly strung.

'How's it going?' she asked, when finally he escaped and came over.

'You really don't want to know.' He gave her a tight smile. 'This will go on for ever. At least as long a Spanish wedding.' He rolled his eyes. 'Just without the dancing.'

Then he looked right at her.

'Can we talk?'

'Of course.'

'Not here.' He pointed across the lavish courtyard. 'My office maybe?'

'Sure.'

She said it more casually than she was feeling, and nervously walked with him up several flights of stairs.

It was a stunning old building and his office was grand, with views over Jerez.

'You shouldn't have come.'

He said it so tersely that Anna flinched, wondering for a second if he was cross with her for turning up—for outing them, even though he'd never minded before, but then he added.

'But I'm very glad you did.'

Her eyes snapped to his, and precisely what was meant by his look Anna couldn't tell, but she saw they were blazing, angry and in agony.

She had never crossed a room so fast in her life. She moved as if to catch him—only he wasn't falling, because he met her halfway.

His kiss was fierce, rough and passionate, as if

all the emotion of the past days was pouring from his lips, and she kissed him back just as hard. Blotting out everything, just offering escape.

Rough kisses crushed all incoming thought. She could feel his hands lifting her, unnecessarily, because she was already scaling him, wrapping herself around him—but not in the way she had the morning before.

This wasn't about comfort…just a final escape.

'Anna…'

Maybe the barrels below were exploding in the cellar? Or perhaps everything was falling apart in the courtyard below? But they were escaping together.

She felt her knickers tear and heard the rapid unbuckling of his belt. It was more than raw. It was necessary and urgent…

For them both.

He took her away from sorrow, as he had the very moment they'd met. He took her to a place Anna did not know.

She wanted his passion unleashed.

This was all they would ever be—she knew it even as she succumbed. It was nothing for him but sex and dark passion. She didn't care in this moment. She only cared that he had needed her and she had been there for him, and he needed her again now, but in a different way—and she needed him too.

She ground onto him as he thrust hard, but then

he took over and she felt the demand of his hands, moving her hips faster. Whatever he gave, he drew out from her, because soon she was reaching a blinding climax and she felt electric in his arms.

His groan as he shot into her was almost reluctant.

She couldn't breathe properly.

Their foreheads were pressed together, and neither wanted to go back down and face reality.

'Can we stay up here?' Sebastián said, and he kissed her face.

She managed a little laugh. 'I wish!'

'When do you go back?' he asked as he lowered her down. 'Tonight?'

'A couple of days,' Anna said, straightening her dress, unable to look at him or even to speak…because he didn't need to hear how much she loved him on this day.

Or ever.

'A couple of days?' he checked.

She could hear a thousand questions in his voice.

One of her shoes had fallen off and she was slipping it back on as he sorted out his suit.

'I can stay in Jerez tonight,' Anna said, 'if you want me to. I have to be back in Marbella tomorrow.'

'Hold on…' He closed his eyes. 'You didn't just fly in for the day?'

'No.'

'What about Willow?'

'She's in Marbella.'

'What?' His voice was like the crack of a whip.

'Sebastián…' Anna kept her voice steady. 'It's fine. She's with Emily and a nanny.'

'No. No…' His eyes were like black saucers. 'Anna…?'

He knew how impossible it must have been for her to make this happen.

Knew that she'd blown up her life to be here for him.

He was thinking of her daughter, here in another country, perhaps upset and confused.

And he was trying to tell himself that funerals were not the best place to make decisions.

Nor for knee-jerk reactions.

'You need to go to her,' he said.

'Sebastián, I wouldn't have left her if I didn't know she was happy and safe.'

'No.' He shook his head. 'You need to go and be with your daughter.'

'We've just—'

She bit her lip so hard he thought she might have drawn blood. They had just had sex—the most intimate of sex—and he was telling her to get the hell out.

'Anna…' He was adamant. 'You need to go back to Willow.'

CHAPTER SEVENTEEN

THE PERILS OF SPAIN, Anna thought as sat on a sun-bed in her bikini, watching Dali and Willow playing in the sea. She must stop having passionate sex the moment she had someone to look after Willow!

Dali had insisted on staying for the full twenty-four hours that Anna had paid her for. And it was perhaps just as well, because she felt dreadfully unravelled.

Sebastián did that to her, though.

Her emergency fund was practically gone, and she was undoubtedly in trouble with her parents. And Emily would be giving her *I told you so* eyes the next time she visited because, despite her brave words, Anna knew she was going to howl to her friend when she saw him with some gorgeous su-permodel.

Yet even if she could go back she wouldn't change a thing.

Or would she…?

Should she have not gone yesterday?

She didn't regret it.

It was more that now she had to mourn the end of what they'd had…

'There you are.

She heard his voice and was startled, hoping he couldn't read her thoughts. She looked up and tried not to burn in a blush.

He was still in his funeral suit and unshaven. He was fully dressed, in a suit, on a beach, and she was the one melting and trying not to show it.

She wanted to leap up and fall into his embrace, or to kiss him or…

But Willow was here.

Or was she just hiding behind her daughter, and actually it was her heart that couldn't handle it?

'Willow's loving the beach,' Anna explained, watching her daughter running in the shallows. 'And Dali insisted on staying because I'd already paid her for a full twenty-four hours.'

'You paid her? I thought—'

'She's *my* daughter,' Anna said. 'And I don't expect my friends to fund—' She blushed. 'Well, if I had stayed away last night…' She tore her eyes away.

His rejection had hurt. And yet it was a pain she had invited in. No, she didn't feel used, although spending last night alone had told her she was not as brave and sure in this as she'd insisted to Emily or to her mother.

Love had got her on that plane.

Love had seen her follow him up those stairs to his office and wrap herself around him.

And he would never want it.

Sebastián spoke. 'I was thinking yesterday that I am just like my mother. Cold and—'

'You're not.'

'Sometimes I am,' he said.

'Sometimes you have to be,' Anna answered.

She was thinking of herself. Thinking how hard it was going to be in the future…visiting her friend, keeping things polite between them. Because she couldn't drag her heart through this again. She would have to learn from him and be cold too.

'Sebastián…' She took a sip of lukewarm water from her plastic bottle and wondered how to say what she had to. 'I'm going to be bringing Willow here in the future…'

'I know.'

'I don't want to confuse her.'

'Of course not—but in what way do you mean?'

'"Mummy's friend came to the beach in a black suit…"'

She watched him give a small smile and then she looked away. She stared at the beautiful blue ocean and listened to the laughter in the air, felt the breeze in the glorious, beautiful moment—and yet there was one thing missing.

'You see, I want to kiss you,' she admitted.

'I'd like that,' he said. 'But you won't do it.'

'No.'

'And I like it that you won't,' Sebastián said. 'I like it that you put Willow first. What did you tell her about coming here? That it was to see the baby?'

'No, I told her my friend had lost his father.'

Her eyes sparkled with the effort of trying to keep the love she felt for him locked in her heart, hidden from everyone. She was exhausted by constantly calling him a friend. There was no one in the world she'd have done this for—except perhaps Emily.

'What about your parents?' he asked.

'The same.' She gave a tight shrug. 'I asked them to bring her out, but no. It's fine. She's having a great time.'

'Is she still speaking Scottish?'

'Spanish now.' Anna smiled. 'How was the rest of last night?'

'Pretty grim,' he said. 'I had to tell Carmen that Maria has been left the family home. I promised her we'd fight it.'

Anna looked out at the ocean, trying not to let him see that it hurt her that he'd rather face all that alone than with her.

'Oh, and I was wrong,' he added. 'There *was* dancing. Maria kicked things off. In my father's memory, of course…'

'She really can't help herself, can she?'

'No.' He sat down on the lounger beside her. 'Anna, it was hell…'

'It sounds it.'

'No, growing up with her, I mean. She left, and then came back, then left again. I think I was eight when I swore off marriage for life.'

'I can see why…'

'So if we do this, then we have to do it right.'

She frowned.

'*I* have to do this right,' he said. 'Because the most important person in this isn't either of us.' He nodded to where Willow was playing. 'Could you see her being happy here?'

'Here?'

'Well, in Jerez. Because we need to know what we want before we tell her...'

'Tell her?'

'I love you, Anna, and it would seem we're no longer a secret.'

'Then why did you send me away?' she flared. 'You're grieving and upset. Please don't say you love me if you're going to take it back tomorrow morning.'

'I love you.'

She knew that tone, and her eyes flew to his. If anyone else had heard his terse words they might think the delivery odd, but she knew him better.

That abrupt tone was calming to her heart.

His decision was made.

'I don't think it's a complete guess that you feel the same. I don't think you'd be here otherwise— and certainly not with Willow. I had time to think last night. Look, I know I'm not ideal father material... I mean, I'm not brilliant with children...' He grimaced. 'I don't know any.'

'I happen to think you're brilliant with children,' Anna said. 'And with teenagers and troubled young women.' She looked at him. 'You told your father what I said about Carmen's riding?'

'He would have said the wrong thing otherwise. But he always steps up in the end. *Stepped*.' He closed his eyes.

'I think you've been a parent for a very long time,' Anna said. 'Since the age of ten.'

'Will you marry me, Anna?'

It was so sudden, and it came out of nowhere. And just as she caught her breath there was more.

'And, if you agree, I would like to make Willow an official cousin to Josefa and adopt her.'

He misread her frown.

'Because Alejandro and I are brothers and our children should be cousins.'

'But you've always said you don't want children…'

'I don't want children with anyone other than you.'

'You haven't even met her yet.'

'I haven't met our future children either, and nor have you. But I know we'll love them. I never want Willow to feel she is not just as important.'

He took her breath away.

'What will I do with myself if I don't have things—family—to worry about?'

He gave her a smile in the sunlight. He was nervous, Anna realised. Certain of his love for her, but as yet uncertain of what might happen next.

'We can take it slowly,' he said. 'I have to be here for a while, to make sure Carmen and Maria don't burn the family home down. And then there is the business…'

She laughed, breathless.

'You did say you wanted a big family…' he added.

'I did.'

'Mine are hard work,' he warned. 'We won't foist everyone on Willow until you think she's ready, and we'll have to sort out where we live, but—'

'*Hola!*'

Anna turned at the sound of her daughter's voice and smiled as she approached with Dali, who had taught her a few words of Spanish.

'*Hola!*' Sebastián said. 'You must be Willow.'

'Yes.' She looked up at him. 'Are you Mummy's friend whose daddy died?'

'I am.' He nodded. 'Sebastián. Pleased to meet you.'

Willow stared at him suspiciously for a moment, and Anna watched her clever girl quietly working things out.

Then, 'Are you Mummy's boyfriend?'

Anna watched Sebastián blink at the very direct question, and before he could respond with a carefully constructed denial Anna settled for the truth.

'Yes,' Anna said, and held her breath, waiting for her daughter's response.

'Okay!' Willow said, and then turned to Dali. 'Can we have one more play in the water?'

A laughing Dali took Willow's hand and they both ran off, leaving a rather stunned couple sitting on the sun loungers.

'That went rather too well,' Anna said.

'I never thought I'd be called a boyfriend!'

'We don't have to take it slowly,' Anna turned to him, and reached over and took his hand. 'I love you so much.'

And in a complicated situation, at least one decision was easy.

'My parents will only want Willow for holidays. My family is here. *Our* family.'

'You're sure?'

'I won't tell her today, but, yes, I think so.' She looked at Willow and then back to him. 'It's the right choice.'

'You know that old Chinese saying…'

'Which one?'

She gave a vague frown—a pathetic attempt at a lie, because she still did not want to admit that it had been her screensaver for months, that she knew it off by heart and she read it every morning and again at night. A girl had some pride!

When the shoe fits, the foot is forgotten; when the belt fits, the belly is forgotten; and when the heart is right, 'for' and 'against' are forgotten. No drives, no compulsions, no needs, no attractions: Then your affairs are under control. You are a free man.

'I don't agree with Zhuangzi on everything,' Sebastián mused. 'Certainly there are needs and attractions. But with you…' he looked deeply into her eyes '…the heart is right.'

She nodded.

Her heart felt right too.

EPILOGUE

PUERTO BANÚS *LOVED* a wedding! There were cheers and whistles as the very blushing bride stepped out of the car to walk along the marina to the waiting yacht.

Anna wore a silver shot-silk dress that was high at the front and then dipped at the back.

Willow wore the awful green flamenco dress that Emily had brought back from her first trip to Spain.

And a mantilla.

As well as that she carried a fan and smiled at the cheers and waves of the people.

'I'm so excited,' Anna said—because it wasn't nervousness she felt, just utter joy as she and Emily held Willow's hands as they made their happy way to the boat.

'Welcome aboard,' said a smiling Dante. 'Everything is ready.'

'Thank you, Dante.'

'You look stunning,' he said—and not just to the bride, but to the delighted five-year-old who really was having her day of days and would soon be spending precious time with her grandparents while Anna and Sebastián enjoyed their honeymoon...

It turned out that Anna's parents really did want lots of holidays with Willow! And they'd surprised

Anna by suggesting that instead of having a wedding in the village she and Sebastián should marry in Spain, with her father there to give a blessing.

'We could have Willow for a few nights while you go on your honeymoon,' her mother had said, as Sebastián had sat on their sofa drinking tea, having first asked permission for his daughter's hand from Anna's father.

Anna had never envisaged a honeymoon, and certainly not a wedding on a yacht, but now she relaxed in the cool saloon, sipping icy water beside an impatient Willow.

'How much longer?'

'Too long!' Anna laughed, because she was as impatient as her daughter, but eventually the engines slowed as the yacht reached its destination and the moment she had never thought would be hers was here.

'Good luck,' Emily said, and gave her a hug. 'I'm so happy and…' She moved her head in and whispered, 'I was so wrong about Sebastián.'

'He says the same about you!' Anna said, and they shared a laugh. Friends for ever.

She climbed the steps very carefully, not wanting to make an inelegant entrance, and as she stepped onto the deck she stopped for a moment to take it all in.

Everyone she loved was there: her parents, smiling widely when they saw little Willow, Carmen looking pale but smiling, about to head for America, Alejandro holding a still-tiny Josefa…

And there was one person whom she didn't love…

Maria wore a *lot* of black ruffles and a black lace mantilla, and she held a black fan. However, she wore suitable shoes for the yacht. Sebastián had not cut her out, but he was keeping a close watch.

Even Maria's presence couldn't unsettle Anna today, because she felt as calm as the gorgeous Mediterranean. A beautiful stillness and peace filled her as she took a breath and looked to Sebastián.

Her captain.

The captain of his family and the captain of her heart.

He wore a dark suit and a gunmetal-grey tie, and his buttonhole was lavender from her tiny garden, where she'd sat so many nights, looking at the sky and thinking of Emily's wedding night and how reckless she'd been…

But perhaps she had been wise to follow her heart?

If today proved anything it was surely that.

He smiled as she walked towards him, and then he smiled for a certain little lady who really was the belle of the ball.

'Willow,' he said, 'you're stealing the show!' He turned to his bride and said in a whisper, 'Maria is jealous of a five-year-old.' Then he looked at Anna and he gave her the smile he saved just for her. 'You look wonderful.'

'You do too,' Anna replied.

He was still not a demonstrative man in public, and he would not be reading her poetry any time soon, but his next words were for her alone, and she knew exactly what they meant. She understood that they told her of the deep well of his love for her.

'Anna…' Sebastián took her hands and she had never seen him more serious. His voice was absolutely clear. 'I love you. You have been there for me, and I promise I shall always be there for you. And for Willow.'

And even if the guests wanted more, Anna didn't need it. She knew that she had his love, that he would always be there for the people he loved.

'*Always,*' he emphasised, with such sincerity that it brought tears to her eyes.

'Sebastián…' She took a breath and collected herself. 'Sebastián,' she said again, in a clearer voice. 'You made me smile the very moment I met you…'

She thought back to that day when she had walked out of the airport and smiled at the memories, and thought of all the memories still to be made.

'I will love you for the rest of my life.' She felt his hand tighten around hers and she looked right into his eyes. 'And I can't wait to share that life with you.'

Then her father forgot he wasn't officiating, and gave a long, droning speech before finally giving the blessing.

And then the celebrant read some strange Chinese quote about feet and bellies, and the bemused gathering shot sideways glances at each other.

The newly married couple knew what it meant though.

Sebastián and Anna knew that this was *their* love.

* * * * *

If you fell in love with
Midnight Surrender to the Spaniard
make sure to check out the first instalment in the
Heirs to the Romero Empire trilogy,
His Innocent for One Spanish Night

And don't forget to explore these other
Carol Marinelli stories!

The Italian's Forbidden Virgin
The Greek's Cinderella Deal
Forbidden to the Powerful Greek
The Sicilian's Defiant Maid
Innocent Until His Forbidden Touch

Available now!